"The brakes are gone."

Keith tried the hopeless action one more time. Still nothing. "Call 911."

Amy fumbled with her phone and placed the call. "Okay, now what?"

The fear in her voice rattled him, but he had to keep his attention on the task at hand. He couldn't leave Carter an orphan after he had just found him.

Amy sat up straight and gripped the dashboard. "Can we make it to the straightaway?"

"Not sure. It's still a couple miles from here."

The air whooshed from Keith's lungs at the sight of a large deer carcass in the middle of his path.

"Hold on, Ams." The loose gravel from the tiny shoulder of the road spit from his tires, pulling his vehicle toward the drop-off. He fought for control. The tires held, then slipped too far for him to recover.

"Hold on!" Keith flung his arm in front of Amy in a futile attempt to stop her from whipping forward.

The truck slid on the rocks and careened over the edge.

Amy's scream pierced the air.

Two-time Genesis Award-winner **Sami A. Abrams** and her husband live in Northern California, but she'll always be a Kansas girl at heart. She enjoys visiting her two grown children and spoiling their sweet fur babies. Most evenings, if Sami's not watching sports, you'll find her engrossed in a romantic suspense novel. She thinks a crime plus a little romance is the recipe for a great story. Visit her at www.samiaabrams.com.

Books by Sami A. Abrams

Love Inspired Suspense

Deputies of Anderson County

Buried Cold Case Secrets
Twin Murder Mix-Up

Visit the Author Profile page at LoveInspired.com.

TWIN MURDER MIX-UP

SAMI A. ABRAMS

LOVE INSPIRED SUSPENSE
INSPIRATIONAL ROMANCE

LOVE INSPIRED® SUSPENSE
INSPIRATIONAL ROMANCE

Recycling programs
for this product may
not exist in your area.

ISBN-13: 978-1-335-58796-1

Twin Murder Mix-Up

For questions and comments about the quality of this book, please contact us at CustomerService@Harlequin.com.

Love Inspired
22 Adelaide St. West, 41st Floor
Toronto, Ontario M5H 4E3, Canada
www.LoveInspired.com

Printed in U.S.A.

Hatred stirreth up strifes: but love covereth all sins.
—*Proverbs* 10:12

ONE

Cool air blasted from the car vents. The AC struggled to stay ahead of the rising summer temperatures. Amy Baker maneuvered through the afternoon traffic, whispering a prayer for the millionth time that the person responsible for her sister's death hadn't discovered his mistake: he'd killed the wrong twin.

That error had not only left her with overwhelming guilt and her sister's baby but had forced her into hiding for the past three months, using her mother's maiden name of Jones to stay under the radar of a killer.

Amy tightened her grip on the steering wheel and scanned her surroundings. Situational awareness. Detective Trent Jefferies had drummed it into her when he'd helped her fade into the background.

Her cell phone buzzed in the cupholder. She glanced at the caller ID. Detective Jefferies. Sweat beaded on her forehead. He never contacted her during the day. His check-ins always came in the evenings after he left work. "Trent?"

"Get out of town now!"

The squeal of tires over the phone line ratcheted Amy's nerves. She pushed down the panic attack threatening to overwhelm her. "What's wrong?"

"Don't go home. Just leave!" The frantic tone of the normally calm Detective Jefferies sent chills running down her spine.

She had no choice but to drive past the one-story bungalow she currently called home. The flash of a dark figure in her living room window caught her eye. A whimper escaped her lips. "Someone's in my house!" Her voice skyrocketed. "How did he find me?" Three months of making herself invisible—gone.

"I'm not sure, but I think I asked the wrong questions and led them to you in Jackson." Trent's car door slammed, reverberating in her ears. "Find a place to hide—"

A shot pierced the air.

"Trent!"

The phone went dead.

Tears flooded her eyes. She blinked to clear her vision. *Please, God, don't let Trent die because of me.*

Mind spinning, she sped from the quiet neighborhood she'd found solace in when she moved to Jackson to hide out. What now? Where would she go? She'd given up her friends when she left her childhood hometown of Eagle Bay and hadn't made new ones for fear they'd say the wrong thing to the wrong person.

She'd tried to call her childhood friend Keith Young when this whole thing started, but he hadn't returned her calls. In fact, he'd ignored her for the past year. His silence had stung, and she had no idea what she'd done to deserve the cold shoulder.

Thankfully, Eagle Bay Police Detective Jefferies had come to her rescue and had hidden her in plain sight in Jackson, a town thirty minutes from her home, away from the person who wanted to kill her. Over the past few months, Trent had become a trusted friend. She had no one else—no family, no other friends. Her parents had died in a car accident years ago, and Amy's twin sister had died in her place. If Trent died, who could she turn to? Trust?

Keith.

Blood whooshed in her ears as she aimed her car out of town toward Keith's new home of Valley Springs, where he worked as a detective with the Anderson County Sheriff's Department.

She glanced in the rearview mirror at her four-month-old nephew. Her heart twisted like a pretzel. What choice did Amy have if she wanted to keep Carter safe but to take another chance on the man she'd secretly loved since she was twelve? Would he answer her call for help? Or would he ghost her once again?

Uncertainty bubbled inside. Amy smacked the heel of her hand against the steering wheel. Why hadn't he been there for her the first time? She knew his mom had fought cancer for the past two years, but that was no excuse to ignore her. When Detective Jefferies gave her a new phone number and requested she not make contact with anyone until he figured out who had killed her sister, she'd stopped her attempts to contact Keith and let the hurt fester. Now she needed him in a big way and prayed he wouldn't let her down—again.

Carter's cries intensified from the back seat. She'd picked him up from daycare and had arrived before he'd had his bottle. With the threat looming, he had to wait until she found a safe place to lie low. Her heart broke for the little guy, but his safety came before satisfying his hunger needs.

"Hold on, baby." Amy turned onto the main road out of town. She prayed the cops wouldn't stop her for speeding. A piece of hair flipped across her face, compliments of the air conditioner. She tucked it behind her ear and focused on the road.

A month ago, after a scare that the person who'd killed her twin had discovered Amy's whereabouts, Trent advised her to pack a bag for herself and Carter and leave it in the trunk of her car. Along with several thousand dollars in cash in case the need to escape arose. It looked as though her past had caught up with her, and Trent had been right. A vise tightened on her chest. She'd lost her sister, become responsible for a newborn and left her treasured job as a professional landscape photographer to hide from a killer all in one horrible moment. And now she had no idea the fate of Trent.

She bit her lip. Why had she gone to take pictures at the cliff overlooking Eagle Lake that afternoon? She could have picked any other time. But no, she had to go that day and witness a woman being shot and falling over the precipice. Tears pricked her eyes. *Why, God?*

Trees lined the highway, and the green grass along the shoulder blurred as she passed. The mileage sign whipped by. Twenty-three miles to Valley Springs. Amy's eyes darted to the side mirrors for the umpteenth time. The cars on the two-lane road had thinned, and no one had followed her. At least to her knowledge.

Carter's cries hit an ear-piercing level. She draped her arm over the back of the seat and reached into his car seat, blindly fumbling for his pacifier. Several attempts later, her fingers found the item. Popping the rubber binky in his mouth, with a singsong voice, she continued soothing her nephew—no, according to Stacey's wishes in her living trust, Amy would raise him as her own child. Amy had signed the final papers yesterday and had yet to crack into the manila envelope stamped *For Amy's Eyes Only* that the attorney had handed her.

Several minutes later, the little man in the car seat settled into a soft whimper.

Her heart ached at the sad sound, and the desire to stop and comfort him flooded her. She had no option but to continue on. Her life and Carter's depended on finding Keith. Terror filled her veins. What if he refused to help? Where would she turn then? No. Keith was a man of honor, and even though she hadn't spoken with him in over a year, she considered him a friend, no matter how bad his silence hurt.

Fingers trembling, she pressed Keith's number on her cell phone and put it on speaker. She prayed he would answer since she'd changed her number months ago at Detective Jefferies's urging.

"Young." Keith's deep timbre filtered across the line, soothing her frayed nerves.

"Keith, it's Amy." She swallowed, forcing down bile. "Someone's after me."

Silence.

Panic gripped her throat, cutting off her ability to breathe. *Please don't turn your back on me. I need you.*

"Keith? Are you there?" She choked out the words. "I need your help before they kill me."

Cell phone to his ear, Detective Keith Young stepped into the sheriff's station parking lot after his shift. His fingers tightened around the device. Amy's words stopped him midstride.

His head spun. Amy had disappeared after Stacey's murder three months ago, and to his surprise, she hadn't contacted him. Granted, he'd ignored her previous attempts at communication over the past year after his glaring blunder with her twin, but after Stacey's death, he'd put aside his personal discomfort and had tried to call. Her phone number had no longer been in service. He rubbed his forehead, chasing away his confusion. "I'm here. Why do you think that?"

"There's stuff you don't know. The reason I haven't called and…well…other things."

A copy of her twin's cold case file sat in the bottom drawer of his desk, haunting him on a daily basis. His mind created a mental picture of the murder scene. Stacey's riffled-through and tossed-aside purse and empty camera bag. A bullet hole in her head and her partially burned body from the killer's attempt to torch the car. Now Amy was in trouble. If he had found God before his stupid choices, maybe his best friends would be safe and by his side.

Regret smashed into him. He and Stacey had made a mistake after a night of celebrating—they'd never told Amy. Not only had his actions damaged his and Stacey's relationship, but calling Stacey by her twin's name had placed a boulder between them. Then he'd pulled away from Amy out of shame, distancing himself by not calling and texting, but he'd never stopped being her friend. Or Stacey's, for that matter. It had just made things more complicated. "Enlighten me."

"I'm about five miles outside of Valley Springs, coming from Jackson. I can meet you—" Amy's muffled cry filled his ears.

"What's wrong?" His voice raised in volume, and his feet pounded a rapid rhythm on the ground.

"He found me!"

"Hold on, Ams. I'm on my way!" He didn't know who was after her, but obviously Amy was in danger. Keith jumped in his truck, mashed on the accelerator and flipped down the visor light bar. Alternating blue and red lights flashed on his front windshield. Pebbles spit from his tires, and the bed of his vehicle fishtailed on the loose gravel. The squeal of rubber pierced the air when he hit the blacktop. "I need your car type and color." His pulse rate increased at her lack of response. "Amy?" Right now, he didn't care about the past. He had to get to her.

"Dark red SUV. Please hurry." Her plea was barely above a whisper.

Keith searched the road. "I should see you any moment." *Come on. Come on.* There. Ahead. He spotted Amy's car a second before a large black truck slammed into the rear of her vehicle, sending her careening off the road.

Her scream sliced the air. The SUV hit the embankment, and the call went dead.

"Amy!" Keith slammed on the brakes and skidded to a stop. He yanked his SIG Sauer from his holster and leaped from his truck.

The offending vehicle spun out and raced off in the opposite direction. He wanted to go after the person responsible, but Amy's well-being took priority.

Feet striking the hard ground, Keith sprinted to the driver's side of Amy's car. Steam hissed from the engine. Heart pounding, he took in the condition of the wrecked vehicle and released a pent-up breath—no immediate fire danger.

He peered through the broken window and sucked in a breath. Amy's blond hair draped over the crimson-stained deflating airbag as she slumped against the black leather steering wheel.

Fingers to her carotid artery, he almost collapsed with relief when her heartbeat met his fingertips. "Amy? Can you hear me?"

She tilted her head to face him, and her unfocused eyes fluttered open. "Keith."

The air whooshed from his lungs. Stacey's vacant eyes stared at him.

He placed a hand on the hood of the car to steady himself. No, not the woman—his friend's—lifeless picture from the file, but her twin, Amy. He had to pull it together. Clearing his throat, he tugged at the phone in his pocket. "Take it easy. I'm calling for an ambulance."

"Keith." Her breathy words worried him. "Baby… Stacey…help." Her head drooped, and eyes closed. Blood trickled from her nose and dripped from a gash on her forehead.

Baby? His mind scrambled to keep up.

Cries broke through his tunneled focus. He glanced in the back seat. A car seat stole the air from his lungs. When had Amy had a baby? If Keith had manned up and not cowered from the shame, he'd have known about her pregnancy. He would have been there to support her. Instead, he stood there like a stranger staring at his best friend's child.

He dialed dispatch and scanned the area for any sign that the person responsible for running her off the road had returned. Satisfied danger didn't lurk around the corner, he yanked open the back door and crawled in next to the crying infant dressed in a dinosaur shirt that screamed *boy*. "Hey, buddy. It's okay. I'm going to get you out of here."

"Dispatch."

"Sonja, it's Keith. I need an ambulance. Highway twelve, two miles outside of town. Look for my truck. And put a BOLO out for a black Ford F-150 heading in the direction of Jackson."

The young dispatcher relayed the information to the fire department and turned her attention back to him. "You okay?"

"I'm fine. A woman and infant were run off the road."

"The guys are on the way."

"Thanks, Sonja." Keith hung up and took a closer look at the baby. No visible injuries, but he'd let Ethan and Brent assess the little dude. Checking the edges of the car seat, Keith found a pacifier and stuck it in the boy's mouth.

Tiny sapphire eyes, identical to Amy's, stared back at Keith. Little fingers gripped his pinkie while the baby's mouth sucked hard on the rubber pacifier. "It's okay, little guy. Help will be here soon." As if on cue, the ambulance siren whined in the distance. "See, here come my friends."

The boy stopped sucking and smiled behind his binky.

"Well, aren't you a happy one." Keith's stomach clenched. He'd dodged the baby bullet the night he and Stacey had crossed the line of friendship. They'd both had too much to drink, and one thing had led to another. He regretted his behavior and the wedge it had placed between him and Stacey, and due to his guilt, he'd pulled away from Amy, as well. Looking into the child's trusting eyes, he vowed to protect Amy from whoever had caused the crash.

"Hey, man, whatcha got there?" Brent slapped him on the back.

Keith crawled from the back seat and proceeded to inform the paramedics what had happened. While the two men treated a semiconscious Amy and her son and loaded them into the ambulance, he gathered Amy's purse, diaper bag and an important-looking envelope from inside the car along with bags from the trunk, then tossed them in the cab of his truck.

Burned rubber and the sickening sweet smell of antifreeze tickled his nose. The mixture was enough to turn his stomach. He swallowed hard and prayed the scent would dissipate soon. Leaning against his truck, he folded his arms across his chest and waited for backup. Duty demanded he remain at the scene, but his heart ached to follow the ambulance to the hospital.

Gravel popped from under the medic truck as it flipped a U-turn and headed toward Valley Springs General Hospital.

Moments later, Deputy Lewis arrived to secure the scene. Keith jogged to the department vehicle and relayed the information to the deputy, then rushed back to his truck, hopped in and sped toward his childhood friend.

The cream-colored walls of the waiting room closed in on Keith, and the hum of the florescent lights grated on his nerves. Amy's words rolled around in his brain. Why had someone attacked her on the highway, and what didn't he know about Stacey's death? His gaze flipped to the door leading to the room that held the woman he had known longer than any of his friends. What had happened to her over the past few months? Obviously, Amy was in danger, but without knowing why or from whom—how could he keep her safe?

The doctor who had examined Amy's baby appeared, pronounced the boy healthy and handed the little guy to Keith.

Keith stared at the doctor. "Wait. Why are you giving him to me?"

"Ms. Baker regained consciousness for a moment in the ambulance and made the paramedic pull out his phone and record her request of giving you custody until she could talk to you."

"Me?"

The man nodded. "And since you're the law around here…" The doctor shrugged and walked away.

Keith lowered himself onto the plastic waiting room chair and snuggled the small bundle. He was honored Amy had such faith in him, especially after his yearlong lack of communication, but he had no clue what to do with a baby.

"Heard you had a new partner and that the kid was hungry." Keith's friend and partner, Jason Cooper, held out a bottle and towel. "Here. I heated it for you."

Keith threw the towel over his shoulder and offered the bottle to the cutie in his arms. He hoped he hadn't gotten it wrong. He was going off how he'd seen the new moms from church bottle-feed their little ones. "Since when do you know anything about babies?"

A mischievous smile formed on Jason's lips. "All right, I confess, one of the nurses helped me."

Keith chuckled. "That's what I thought."

His partner's teasing grin faded. "Security is standing watch, and I asked Janie to keep an eye on our victim. Told her to come get us if there was trouble."

"The nurse who treated Melanie?" He yanked down the towel and dabbed the dribble of formula from the baby's chin.

"Same."

Not long ago, Jason's fiancée had run into trouble, and the pair had racked up frequent flyer miles at the hospital.

The tension in Keith's shoulders eased. At least someone had eyes on Amy if he couldn't.

Jason lowered himself into the chair next to him. "Want to tell me what's going on?"

"I would if I could." Keith tossed the cloth onto his shoulder. "All I know is that Amy called, scared, and the next thing I know, she's on her way to Valley Springs and is forced off the road."

"Is she the one from your hometown?"

Keith nodded. "She and her twin sister were my best friends growing up." Until he messed things up with Stacey and ignored Amy out of guilt. He wondered if Amy knew about his and her twin's poor choices. Heat flooded his cheeks. Would he ever let go of the embarrassment from his actions?

"And the baby?"

He lifted the little guy to his shoulder and patted his back. "Hers, I assume. Looks like her anyway." Of course, the infant looked like Stacey, too. The kid had to be about three or four months old. He did the math in his head. His pulse raced. No way. Stacey would have told him.

"Carter!"

His gaze flew to Amy. Bruises covered her face, and an angry red cut marred her forehead.

A nurse brought Amy's wheelchair into the room and stopped a few feet from Keith. Amy pushed herself to a standing position and swayed.

"Whoa. Sit down. I'll bring him to you." Keith stood and transferred Amy's son into her arms.

She placed a kiss on top of the infant's head. "Thank you." Tears brimmed her lashes. "I don't know what I would've done if something happened to him."

Keith had questions, and he wanted answers—now. But instead of pushing her about the incident, he crouched to eye level and asked, "Are you okay?"

"I—" The automatic door whooshed open and with it came the humid summer air. Her eyes widened, and she wrapped Carter protectively in her arms.

He shot to his feet and flipped open the snap on his holster. Hand hovering over the butt of his weapon, he stepped in front of Amy and faced the door. A rush of air escaped his lungs. Another patient walked in and checked in with the receptionist.

He pivoted and returned his attention to Amy. "Let's get you out of here so you can rest. Then you need to tell me what's going on."

Amy bit her lip at his harsh tone. Her gaze dropped to the floor, and she nodded.

Keith felt like a heel, but frustration had dug in its claws.

"I'll bring your truck to the door." Jason grabbed Keith's keys and slipped from the room.

"I don't know how to thank you." Amy's voice shook.

She could thank him by telling him things about Stacey's death and why she was in trouble. But he knew from experience, if he wanted her to talk, he had to choose his words carefully. She had a stubborn streak and didn't take kindly to demands. "Don't worry about it. Let's just get you somewhere safe. Then we can figure this out."

Jason arrived and assisted Amy into the passenger seat while Keith struggled to secure Carter into the car seat that Jason picked up at the store since the one from the accident couldn't be safely used anymore. Sweat trickled down between Keith's shoulder blades as he secured the safety device.

His partner closed the door and slapped him on the back. "Let me know when you figure out what you need."

"Will do. Thanks, man." Keith slid into the driver's seat and shifted to face Amy.

She leaned her head back and closed her eyes. "I'm in trouble."

Concern coiled in Keith's stomach. Amy was in danger. Stacey's lifeless body flashed through his mind. He refused to let the same thing happen to Amy.

TWO

"Are you sure you won't let me find you somewhere else to stay other than a hotel?" Keith delivered the bag and personal items he'd collected from Amy's car to her room.

"Carter and I are good." Amy held the baby close and lowered herself onto the dark green easy chair in the small living room. "You didn't have to reserve a suite for us. I can't afford this room for more than tonight." The crease on Amy's forehead deepened.

Keith placed her laptop bag on the desk then knelt before her. "Don't worry about the money. I've got this."

"Keith…"

"No argument. That's what friends are for." He stuck out his index finger, and Carter wrapped his tiny hand around it. "Besides, champ here needs his space."

She chuckled, then winced. "He's four months old, not a teenager."

"Still. I want to help." Guilt plagued him. He'd ignored Amy's calls for the past year out of humiliation. After Stacey's death, he'd laid his mother to rest, but he should've pulled himself out of his own grief and supported Amy. At least he had his father. She had no one. With her parents' deaths and now Stacey's murder, Amy had no family to speak of. By the time Keith had been ready to talk, she'd disappeared. No forwarding address or phone number.

Her mouth twisted to the side. "For now. Having the room in your name adds a layer of security." She raised her gaze to meet his. Worry lined her features. "Thank you."

"You're welcome." Keith stood, pulled the curtain open an inch and peeked out. The detective in him screamed to sit Amy down and force the story out of her, but he knew better. She'd clam up or give him vague information. Not because she'd refuse to tell him, but the more he pushed, the more she'd pull, simply out of instinct.

The air conditioner kicked on and hummed in the background. He blinked away his annoyance and focused on the parking lot. Five cars plus his truck. Everything appeared peaceful, but he wasn't banking on it staying that way. He dropped the cloth and made a mental note to call Valley Springs PD and ask them to send patrols by the hotel when he wasn't available to stand guard. Sauntering to the door, he picked up the portable crib the hotel staff had supplied. "Let me see if I can get this thing set up before little man goes to sleep."

"I can take care of that." The fatigue lacing Amy's features said otherwise. "You've done so much for us."

"I've got this. You have orders to rest." He turned the contraption in his hands. How in the world did the thing work?

Laughter bubbled from Amy. "Would you like some help?"

The sound of her merriment eased the tightness in his chest. He'd always loved her cheerful nature. "Nah. Just give me a minute." He scratched the stubble on his jaw. You apparently needed a college degree to figure out the crazy thing. Maybe he should turn in his man card. *Ah ha.* Keith pushed the center piece down, and the sides popped open. Now to lock the dumb thing into place. He narrowed his gaze looking for the answer.

"Try turning the handle in the middle."

He followed Amy's instructions, and the crib took shape. "There."

"I knew you could do it." She smiled.

Hands on his hips, he gave her a teasing glare. "Yeah, right. You were enjoying my struggle."

"Maybe a little." She pinched her lips together,

masking her amusement. But her eyes told a different story.

Amazing how quickly they eased back into their old ways, but he knew she felt the wedge between them like he did. Her expression held a distance that had never existed before. One he wanted to erase, but changing the past—impossible. He turned his attention to the task at hand and padded the crib with the included mattress, then rummaged through the diaper bag and extracted a blanket. "You think…" He raised his gaze and stopped.

"Shh…he's asleep." Amy wiggled out of the chair and grimaced as she stood. "Let me put him down." By her stilted movements, her muscles had stiffened.

"Can I help?"

"Nah. Give me a minute. I think the accident is catching up with me." She lowered Carter into his new bed and tucked him in. "He should be out for the night." She placed her hand on the edge of the crib and struggled to straighten.

He grabbed her elbow and helped her to an upright position.

"Thanks." Amy rubbed her lower back.

Keith wanted to pull her into a hug and apologize for everything he'd done to mess up their friendship, but instead, he kept the words from falling from his lips and glanced at his watch.

He'd allowed her time to get settled, and now he needed answers. "Do you have enough energy to give me the CliffsNotes version of what happened?" Without giving her the opportunity to say no, he motioned to the couch. "Why don't you stretch out. I'll take the chair."

She sighed and sat on the sofa. Stuffing a pillow behind her back, she reclined and stretched her legs in front of her on the cushions.

Time to get down to business. He'd tempered his frustration long enough to get Carter settled. Elbows on his knees, Keith blew out a breath. "What's going on, Amy?" His words were harsher than he'd intended. He softened his tone. "Stacey might have been the daredevil twin, but you've always had an adventurous nature. You might be the shy one, but you've never backed down from a fight." His gaze met hers. The woman in front of him was frightened and unsure of herself. Not the Amy he knew. "You have to tell me what happened."

Terrified blue eyes stared at him. "I killed Stacey."

The air whooshed from his lungs. The image of Stacey with a bullet hole in her forehead and her partially burned body flashed in his mind. How? Why? He opened his mouth, but the words refused to form. He couldn't wrap his mind around her confession.

No way Amy had ended her twin's life. Keith shook his head, but her words hovered like a thick fog. As her friend and local law enforcement, he had to ask. He scrubbed his face with his hands and cleared the lump in his throat. "You shot her and set fire to her car?"

"No!" Amy softened her voice as not to wake Carter. "No, I didn't shoot her or start the fire." Not exactly what she'd meant, but Amy was responsible just the same as if she'd pulled the trigger. "But the thug killed the wrong twin. That bullet had my name on it, not Stacey's."

Amy watched as Keith pushed from the chair and ran a hand through his hair.

His shoulders tensed. "Why would someone want to kill you? And why was Stacey killed by mistake?"

He could *not* be serious. Amy raised a brow. "Hello. Identical twin."

"Yeah, yeah, dumb question."

Amy's insides coiled as he paced circles in the small living room. Irritation poured off him. She grabbed his hand and stopped his movement. "Please. Sit down. You're making me jumpy."

With a nod, he dropped into the chair. His hair stuck up in odd angles giving him that cute young boy look she remembered from her childhood. The one that stole her heart years ago.

"Sorry. But Ams, you should have told me. We needed to know for the investigation. You've kept vital information from me."

She gritted her teeth. Giving up her life and hiding for the past three months to stay alive didn't count for anything? "Really? After going dark for an entire year, you expected me to confide in you?" Careful of her injuries, she massaged her temples. She attempted to rein in her irritation but was unsuccessful. "I tried to contact the sheriff's office, but they said you were out on leave. I didn't know who to trust." Her voice rose. Amy had needed him, but the unanswered phone calls had crushed her. Her fingers gripped the throw pillow, and she hugged it to her chest. Taking a breath, Amy forced herself to soften her tone. The last thing she needed was for Carter to wake up.

"This whole mess started three months ago when I lived in Eagle Bay." Amy played with the tassel on the pillow. Her hands trembled. She could do this—had to do this. She was tired of hiding and wanted her sister's murderer caught. "Stace was home on leave before her deployment, so she took care of Carter while I headed out and hiked up Eagle Ridge above Shadow Lake. The scenery there is breathtaking, ya know. The sun glistening off the snow framed by the icy trees and lake in the distance beyond the rocks. The perfect winter paradise shot. I wanted to include several landscape photos of the overhang in my next art show."

Oh, how she missed her career as a professional landscape photographer. She'd worked hard to make a name for herself. Biting her lip, she shook her head. Some day she hoped to go home, but until the police put the man who murdered her sister behind bars, she refused to return and risk her or Carter's life.

"Anyway, I had climbed the trail and found a great spot. I'd taken dozens of pictures when I panned to the cliff for the money shot." The corner of her mouth hitched. True, the perfect picture would have netted her thousands, but the pure awe from the art community she would have received warmed her heart. She sighed. That experience had to wait. "That was when I noticed two figures at the rocky edge, so I zoomed in." Eyes closed, her stomach threatened to revolt. The vivid visual replay had never eased any time she allowed her mind to wander back to that horrible moment.

"Ams?"

Her lids popped open, and she inhaled through her nose, willing the bile down. "I'm fine."

"You sure 'bout that? You could audition for Morticia's double."

Leave it to Keith to notice. She ignored his

reference to *The Addams Family* and continued. "A young woman with auburn hair struggled against a tall, hooded figure. I couldn't see the man's face." She sucked in a whimper. "It all happened so fast. I pushed down the shutter release button on my camera and let it auto take pictures on burst mode. When he pulled out a gun and shot the girl, she tumbled over the side of the cliff. I screamed, but it was too late." The gunshot and her own scream plagued her sleep most nights. Waking up in a cold sweat was a common occurrence. She relished the day when the past wouldn't invade the present.

Keith leaned forward, placed his elbows on his knees and gave a quick nod, encouraging her to continue.

Bottom lip between her teeth, she slumped her shoulders. "Whoever killed the woman turned in my direction. I ran down the trail to the parking lot and got out of there. But not before he made it to the trailhead and spotted my car."

"Go on."

"Once I got home, I popped the SD card from my camera and ran into the house. I'd left my cell phone on my dresser. I had a free afternoon and hadn't wanted to be disturbed while I worked." A mistake she'd never make again. "I hurried to my room to call 9-1-1. Stace must have seen me come home. Her car was already in storage, and she'd asked to borrow mine after I came back from my photo shoot. Said she had unfinished business in Valley Springs that she had to take care of. When I came out of the bedroom, the extra set of keys were gone from the basket and so was my car."

"So, you called the Eagle Bay police about the incident on the cliff? What did they say?" His concerned blue-gray eyes pierced her heart.

"That they'd check it out and have someone from the Anderson County Sheriff's Department call me back since it was out of Eagle Bay PD jurisdiction."

"Who'd you talk to at county?"

"No one. They never called."

His jaw dropped. "What?"

No one had called her back about a murder? She had to be mistaken. Although, come to think about it, Keith didn't recall a death investigation that matched her description and date. Of course, he'd dealt with his mother's funeral around that time and had taken a couple of weeks off.

"Since Stacey died on the county road, ACSD notified me that night about her death but had only told me it was a car accident with suspicious circumstances. Later, I found out that someone shot her and tried to burn the car with her inside. 'Suspicious circumstances' was an understatement. At first, I had no idea that it connected to what I'd seen. After a couple weeks and still no one had contacted me about the woman who died on the cliff, and since I called 9-1-1 in Eagle Bay, I went to the EB police station, where I met Detective Jefferies. He couldn't find any record of my original call. I had planned to give him the SD card, but something felt off, so I kept my mouth shut and started to leave. Trent—Detective Jefferies—stopped me and handed me his business card." Amy wiped a stray tear from her cheek. "When I got to my car and had Carter buckled in his car seat, I looked at the card and flipped it over. He'd written me a note." She wrapped her arms around her waist and dipped her head.

"What did it say?"

She peered up at him. "He gave me his private number and told me to call in an hour."

That didn't sound good. No police officer doled out his personal cell phone number to a stranger. Keith scooted to the edge of his seat. "And?"

"And he said something weird was going on, and I should lie low while he looked into it."

"That's why you moved from Eagle Bay and hid in Jackson?"

"Yes, but I didn't move right away. Over the next several days, I got to know Trent and trusted him. He was the only one who came to my aid. I tried *other* people, but they didn't respond." Amy pinned Keith with a glare.

He squirmed under her scrutiny. Yeah, okay, so he'd seen her number on his call log a few months ago but had no idea she was in trouble. He would have answered. Should have answered, but he was on leave dealing with his mother's death. *Admit it, Young, you didn't want to face her.*

"I didn't know what to do. So, when Trent told me to leave town, I packed my car with the essentials and checked into a hotel. A few days later, he rented a house for me in Jackson under his stepmom's name, arranged for a new cell phone number and helped me get a temporary job. I settled into my new life. I had given Trent the SD card, and he promised to investigate. He called a few times a week to check on us and update me with any progress." She yawned. "Sorry. Today is catching up with me. Anyway, a couple of days ago, he said he was onto something but never told me what."

"No one investigated the murder?"

"Nope. Only Detective Jefferies at Eagle Bay PD investigated the missing 9-1-1 records, and the lack of communication to Anderson County Sheriff's Department. No one *else* returned my calls."

Wow, if her jabs were firebombs, he'd be burned to a crisp. Keith turned his focus back to her story. His mind spun. How had a murder gone uninvestigated? No way the sheriff's department had let that slip by.

Dark shadows below Amy's eyes spoke of her fatigue, but she continued. "Today, Trent called and told me he'd asked the wrong questions and to get out of town. That's when I heard a gunshot, and the line went dead. I didn't know what else to do, so I came to Valley Springs to find you."

Keith clasped his hands together. Why had she waited until now? "You should have told me sooner."

"Really? I tried. You haven't answered my calls or returned my text messages for a year now." She glared at him. "At least Detective Jefferies had the decency to listen to me and help."

Ouch! She had him there. He'd ignored her out of pride. Months of text messages had gone unanswered. How could he have gone on as if nothing had happened between him and Stacey? Besides, Amy would have known he was hiding something. She'd always been able to tell. But if he'd known about the trouble, he'd have manned up and stood by her side. Right? "You should have found a way to tell me about witnessing a murder."

"Why leave you another message? So you could ignore me again?"

Keith rubbed the back of his neck and counted to ten. Getting his dander up solved nothing. "You could have at least mentioned being pregnant with Carter."

She opened her mouth to respond.

He held out his palm. "I'm just saying, if you'd texted me, I'd have been there for you."

Amy lifted a trembling hand to her forehead. "I...um... Carter isn't mine. He is—was—Stacey's."

Keith's mind scrambled for purchase on the news. Why hadn't Stacey said something? They'd been friends since forever. Yes, he and Stace had one night they'd always regret, but that wasn't a reason to not turn to him when some guy had gotten her pregnant. "I thought... Never mind, it doesn't matter. You obviously love the little guy. May I ask who the father is?" He'd strangle the guy for not stepping up.

She shrugged. "My sister wouldn't tell me. Said it was better that way."

"Surely, Stace put the guy's name on the birth certificate."

"Nope. Not that I know of."

"She had to know who it was. Stacey wasn't the type of girl to sleep around." He knew that one firsthand. He closed his eyes and let the regret wash over him. If he could kick himself, he would. He glanced in the direction of the portable crib. Icy fingers crawled up his back. Could Carter be his? He mentally shook his head. No, Stacey wouldn't have kept that from him. Would she?

"She wasn't." Amy wiped a tear from her cheek. "I've always wondered what happened. I wished she had trusted me. I never understood why. We were twins. Yes, we had our issues, but we shared the important stuff. Or I thought we did." She snuggled into the couch and winced.

"Listen, let's call it a night, and I'll let you get some sleep." As soon as he left, he planned to call his buddy at the office and ask him to look into Amy's report—or lack thereof. Along with the case file on Stacey's death. If the two events were related, they had their first lead in Stace's murder. "Can I get you anything before I go?" He stood and stepped beside her. Holding out his hand, she took it and eased to a seated position.

"I'm good. Carter's a champion sleeper, so I should have another eight hours before he wakes up."

Keith tightened his grip. He hated leaving her alone, but he had no choice if he wanted to investigate her claims. "Be safe, Ams. I'll check the perimeter on my way out."

"Thanks." Her sad smile broke his heart. Why hadn't he stuffed his shame in a box and reached out to her?

"See you in the morning. Sleep well." He peeked in on Carter then meandered to the door. Stepping outside, he inhaled the fresh night air. He scanned the thick woods behind the hotel and the parking lot then glanced at Amy's second-story window. He couldn't leave her without protection now that he knew she'd witnessed a murder. And what was up with that anyway? No follow-up, and as far as he remembered, the department had no record of a gunshot victim at Eagle Ridge. The fact sat like a bad burrito in his gut. He owed Detective Jefferies for keeping Amy safe, assuming the man was still alive. Another thing he'd inquire about.

He yanked the phone from his pocket and dialed his friend Detective Kyle Howard as he slid into the driver's seat of his extended cab truck.

"Howard."

"Hey, Kyle, how's it going at the office?"

"I hate paperwork," the detective groaned.

Keith smothered a chuckle. No officer he knew enjoyed the desk job side of law enforcement. "Enough said." He leaned onto the steering wheel and peered through the front windshield, inspecting the area once more. The tree line beyond the hotel appeared peaceful. His tense muscles relaxed a smidge.

"I know you didn't call to ask me how work was going. What's up?"

On duty, the man had a down-to-business attitude. He liked that about Kyle. "I need information."

"Of course you do." Keith heard the smile in his friend's voice. "Name it."

"Three months ago, is there a record of a homicide at Eagle Ridge?" Keith settled back against the seat after confirming no one lurked along the perimeter of the hotel. He lowered his windows a couple of inches. The evening had cooled, and a slight breeze filtered through his truck. He heard the click of keys as Kyle searched for the report.

"Nada."

"Nothing? You sure about that? It would have been while I was on bereavement leave."

"Nope. Look, man, if we had a suspicious death in that area, they would have pulled you and Jason, or Doug and I, in. I've got zilch. And I don't remember receiving a call either."

Keith rubbed his forehead. He trusted Amy. If she said she'd seen a murder, then it had happened. So why hadn't Eagle Bay PD passed on the information to county? Eagle Ridge landed in ACSD's territory.

"Thanks. Oh, what do you know about a Detective Trent Jefferies?"

"Went to college with him. Solid guy. Works for Eagle Bay PD."

"You trust him?"

"Without a doubt. Why? What's going on?"

That was the first bit of good news he'd heard lately. "Just curious. Trent's name came up, and I felt compelled to ask."

"Riiight."

The man knew him well, but Keith refused to go into detail. At least not yet. "Thanks, Howard."

"Any time. And Young…you'll have to let me know what this is about next time I see you."

"Will do." Keith hung up and stared at his phone. He knew things fell through the proverbial cracks on occasion, but not something this big. He had a bad feeling about the whole situation. And until he found the person responsible for Stacey's death and running Amy off the road, he'd stick close to her and Carter. Even with her hot and cold attitude toward him, she'd have to deal with it. He refused to lose another person from his life.

Grateful the temps had dropped during the evening hours, he locked the doors and reached over the back seat and grabbed his windbreaker. At least he wouldn't swelter in his truck tonight. Unwilling to leave Amy, he bunched the jacket into a ball, leaned against the cooling glass and stuffed the material under his head. His gaze drifted to the hotel window. Memories of his childhood flitted through his mind. The three of them riding bikes, going fishing and other things too numerous to list. He'd been one of the few who could tell the identical twins apart at a glance. They'd tried to fool him a time or two, but he'd always known. Amy had a cute little dimple in her right cheek that Stacey didn't possess. So tiny, people easily missed it. Amy was the sugar to Stacey's spice. And he preferred sugar every day of the week. That's why his poor judgment a year ago hurt so badly. A stupid mistake, and the wrong twin. Then he'd compounded the problem by ghosting Amy. He wanted her forgiveness, but he didn't deserve it. A lump landed in Keith's throat. He'd lost Stacey to a killer who remained at large. He refused to allow anything bad to happen to Amy.

After another scan of the area, he slid down in the seat and crossed his arms over his chest, settling in for a long night.

An odd buzz annoyed him. He brushed at his ear in an attempt to shoo away the pesky fly who'd interrupted his rest. His eyes flew open, and he jerked upright. Not a fly, but his cell phone vibrating in the cupholder.

Keith swiped a hand down his face. How had he fallen asleep when he'd promised himself to watch out for trouble? He grabbed his phone and jabbed the *on* button. "Young."

"Wow, don't sound so happy to hear from me,"

Jason teased on the other end of the line. Since he'd married Dr. Melanie Hutton, his partner's perpetual happiness had made Keith want to walk away from Jason on more than one occasion. But he envied the man for finding someone to share life with.

"What do you want?" Not only grumpy for the abrupt wake-up, he was mad at himself for his lack of ability to stay alert.

"Touchy much?" His partner chuckled. "Had a break-in at the car lot. Someone broke into your friend's car."

Jason had his attention. "Anything taken?"

"Not that I can tell, but whoever did it was looking for something, at least until Duke arrived."

Keith bit back a grin. Duke, the mutt Chad had found on the side of the road and taken in, was the auto shop's mascot and security force. The pup was a friendly guy until you messed with his owner's property, then watch out.

"Did Duke take care of him?" Keith hoped the dog had *taken a bite out of crime* or at least stopped the person who'd broken in.

"Nope. The suspect got away."

Keith sighed. "Of course he did."

"Sheriff Monroe wants you to go take a look since you retrieved Amy's things. He thought you might know if the slime bag took something."

Keith pinched the bridge of his nose. He had no desire to leave Amy alone with her attacker on the loose, and if Jason didn't have to stay and maintain the security of the scene, Keith would've had him switch places. But he'd been careful not to make her whereabouts known, so she should be safe. Only his paranoia had him sitting outside her hotel room. Besides, he had a job to do. He cranked the engine of his truck.

"Not sure I can be of much help, but I'd rather not disturb her unless we have to tonight. I'm on my way." He jabbed the *end* button and placed a call to Valley Springs PD for courtesy patrols by the hotel for the rest of the night. He gave the parking lot and surrounding area one last perusal. Regret wrapped around him like a blanket. *Please, watch over her.*

Keith pulled away from the hotel and pointed his vehicle toward Chad's Auto Body, where the department had an attached impound lot. Each mile that passed twisted his gut. He'd let Amy down once before when she'd needed him. He refused to do it again. He'd keep her safe if it was the last thing he ever did.

The next morning, disappointment settled in Amy's bones as she trudged from the pharmacy across the street back to the hotel. She'd had to leave her home, her sister's killer remained on the loose, and Keith appeared to care enough, but continued to hold her at a distance. Would her life ever settle down, and what had she done to create such a chasm between herself and Keith?

She'd spent her entire life in her twin's shadow, always second best. Never as athletic, smart or outgoing. The only thing she excelled at was photography, but only because Stace had no interest. Amy hid her insecurities well over the years. No one knew about her self-doubt. On the night the three of them celebrated Stace's promotion, Amy had decided she'd push her uncertainty aside and tell Keith how she really felt about him. But that conversation never happened. He'd walked away and ignored her attempts at communication. Had he anticipated her spilling her guts to him, and instead of telling her he wasn't interested in her that way, he'd simply ignored her in hopes she'd get the message? Amy shook the thought from her head. That didn't make sense either. Did it? She blew out a frustrated breath and continued her trek.

Detective Jefferies had texted in the middle of the night, making arrangements to meet her at the hotel at nine this morning. Thankfully, she still had a couple of hours before his scheduled arrival time.

Carter on her hip, she juggled the four bags of items. Diapers, wipes, baby food and a few other necessities filled the sacks. Reaching her door, she fumbled for the key card to her room.

"Little man, you're getting heavy." She kissed his chubby cheek and smiled when she received a toothless grin in return.

She lifted her gaze to the lock. The breath whooshed from her lungs. The door stood ajar. Against her better judgment, she peeked in. Her things lay scattered around the room. Her eyes drifted to the bed. Detective Jefferies's lifeless body draped over the end. Blood pooled on the floor beneath his head.

Swallowing the scream building in her throat, she dropped her purchases, clung to Carter and sprinted to the front office. Her heartbeat hammered against her breastbone. No question in her mind, someone had killed the man because of her. She rounded the corner and slammed into solid muscle.

Strong arms encircled her.

"No. Please, no. Don't hurt him." Amy pivoted Carter away from the man. The baby might not be her biological child, but she'd protect him with her life.

"It's okay, Ams. It's only me."

A familiar woodsy scent filled her senses. "Keith?"

"I'm right here."

She collapsed against his chest and relished

the warmth of his embrace. His hand rubbed up and down her back, soothing her frayed nerves.

"What's wrong?"

"He's dead." The words squeaked past the lump in her throat. "Trent's dead."

"Calm down, Ams. How do you know? Maybe he's got a case and is unable to call."

She shook her head. "N-no. He's in my room. There's so much blood."

Keith tucked her behind him, pulled his weapon and called for backup. "Amy, I want you to go with Mrs. Sterling." He pointed to the silver-haired lady at the front desk. "Nancy, take my friend to the back room and close the door. Don't let anyone in but me. Got that?"

Nancy nodded and rushed to wrap her arm around Amy's shoulder. "Come on, dear. Let's get you and the little one out of here. I have a nice comfy sofa in the back."

She glanced over the older lady's head to Keith as the woman led her to the back room. Oh, how Amy wanted Keith by her side. It didn't matter that they had drifted apart, and he'd hurt her with his silence, but Trent's death deserved Keith's undivided attention. The memory of Detective Jefferies's lifeless body slammed into her. Another senseless death.

When had her life become a series of tragedies? First her parents, then her twin sister and now the man who'd risked his life to keep her safe. When would it end?

"You okay, honey?" The sweet silver-haired lady squeezed Amy's fingers.

No. Not in any form of the word was she okay. A man lay dead in her room. He wasn't supposed to be here yet. Why had he come early? Was she the target? More importantly, how had he gotten into the room?

"Here, have a seat. I'll fix you a little something for breakfast." Nancy hustled to the mini kitchen.

Amy had no desire to eat, but her stomach grumbled in protest to the lack of food.

Nancy placed a white paper plate in front of her filled with a bagel and cream cheese, and fruit. "Can I take that little sweetheart for you?"

Her heart pounded at the thought of handing over her child. Sensing her tension, Carter's body went rigid. She kissed the top of his head and squeezed him tight. "No, that's okay. I think I'll keep him right here."

Mrs. Sterling patted her forearm. "I understand. Nothing like the love of a baby to calm the nerves."

Until she'd signed the papers and took over as Carter's legal guardian after his birth per military requirements, she'd never understood why women held so tightly to their children. But Nancy's words rang true; holding Carter eased her worries.

Amy shifted her bundle and whispered in his ear. "I'm here. No one is going to hurt you. I promise."

He poked his tiny finger in her mouth and grinned.

She held her lips around his finger, then slipped it out of her mouth and kissed the tip. "Go to sleep, sweetie." She rubbed circles on his back and prayed for his safety.

Carter's eyes drooped closed. His long lashes lay over his chubby cheeks. Within minutes his body relaxed, and his breathing slowed.

She shifted his sleeping form and snagged a piece of cantaloupe from the plate. Before Amy realized it, she'd devoured the food, and her mood had improved.

"Better?"

"Oh, sorry." Amy had forgotten she had company in the room. "Yes, thanks. The food helped." Now, if only Keith would come back and tell her she'd imagined the whole thing. But the pool of blood under Trent's head made that wish impossible.

A shiver snaked up her spine, and she tightened her grip on the sweet boy in her arms. What if she hadn't gone to the pharmacy? What if the killer had come into her room and had killed her and Carter while she slept?

Keith's friend and coworker Kyle had shown up and taken charge of the scene. Keith knew, due to his relationship with Amy, the sheriff would hand off the crime to another detective, but Keith planned to stay close. A couple of months ago, Sheriff Dennis Monroe had given all four detectives the freedom to open cold cases as they saw fit. Sure, current investigations were their primary job, but an unsolved crime took center stage from time to time. And right now, Stacey's murder and the person after Amy topped his priority list. He trusted Kyle, but he refused to allow Amy's case to turn cold like Stacey's. There wasn't anything he could do for Stacey, but Amy's life depended on him finding the killer. His mind drifted back to Amy's statement of killing the wrong twin. Were the two cases really connected? If he believed Amy, which at the moment he did, he had to find the person responsible as soon as possible.

Keith stood to the side, allowing Kyle to examine the deceased. "Glad you're here."

"Wish I could say the same." An expression of sadness flashed across Kyle's face.

"Amy said his name's Detective Trent Jefferies from Eagle Bay." Keith halted. "Wait, this is your friend."

Kyle exhaled. "Yup, sure was. At least during college. Haven't seen him in a couple of years."

"You going to be okay doing this? I can call Doug, or Jason, for that matter." The pallor of Kyle's face worried Keith. He remembered wanting to yell and punch something when they'd told him about Stacey's body a few months back.

Kyle shook his head and snapped a few pictures with his phone. "Who found him?"

"Amy. This is her room." Keith crouched on the balls of his feet.

Kyle's eyebrows rose. "Any chance she did this?"

"No," he said, leaving no mistake about his opinion. Keith might have gone radio silent over the past year and missed a few major life events, but no way had she killed Trent.

"You know I had to ask. I can't go off your word alone." Kyle's gaze returned to Jefferies. "How'd Trent end up here?"

"Yeah, I know. And to answer your question, I'm not sure, but he was the one helping her. During her last communication with him, he told her to run. She heard gunshots before the call dropped. That was yesterday. Guess someone got angry about his involvement."

"Good possibility. But that's a fresh bullet

wound, and my guess, the cause of death." Detective Howard pointed to the hole in the side of Trent's head. "That happened today." Kyle stood and arched his back. He jutted his chin at the door. "Why don't you take your friend to the station and grab her statement. I'll finish up here. Once Dr. Hutton-Cooper arrives, I'll have Deputy Lewis monitor the scene, and then I'll join you."

Keith raised a brow. Kyle asked him to get a witness statement? The newly established rivalry between the detective teams might be friendly but crossing over the line brought on serious repercussions. Each team took pride in their work and refused to allow anyone to mess up the reputations they'd built.

"What?"

"Nothing." Not questioning Kyle's offer, Keith stood. "I'll see ya soon." His gaze ran over the room one last time, taking in as many details as possible. He pivoted and exited the crime scene. If he hadn't been called away, would his presence have stopped the murder from happening? The search had taken longer than planned. But Valley Springs PD had texted frequent updates on their drive-bys, so he'd let his guard down and swung by his place for a shower and clean clothes before returning to the hotel. Stupid move on his part.

He strode down the corridor and exhaled, releasing the tension that had settled in his shoulders. What if Amy hadn't left with Carter? Would the killer have eliminated her, too? The thought niggled his brain. He couldn't shake the vision of the trashed room. Like the attacker had searched for something. His steps faltered. He stopped and glanced toward the crime scene. What was this guy's endgame? To find something Amy had, or to kill her? Whatever the person's reason, the maniac had made a pretty bold statement by leaving the body of a dead cop.

He rounded the corner and headed for the front desk. Knuckles on the door to the hotel manager's break room, he knocked. "Amy? It's Keith. Open up."

The door opened a crack, and Amy's piercing blue eyes peered up at him. "He's really dead, isn't he?" Her voice trembled.

"Yes. Detective Jefferies is gone." Keith slipped into the private room.

White washed over Amy's face, and tears welled on her lashes.

He'd thought the detective was a casual acquaintance, but maybe not. And so what if the man had been more. Keith had no reason to be jealous—but yet, the idea gnawed at him. He tucked the odd reaction away to ponder later. "How well did you know him?"

"Not well. Detective Jefferies helped me hide

while he investigated. It's just that…" She bit her lower lip. "I'm sorry he was killed. I can't help but think this is connected to me, and I'm the reason he's dead."

Keith was sure of that. Why else would an officer be found shot to death in her hotel room? But he didn't need to confirm her role. It wasn't her fault, and it would only make her feel worse. "Let's get you to the station. I'll feel better if you're safely tucked away until we figure out what's going on. Besides, Detective Howard—" he jerked his thumb toward the hotel room "—asked me to take your statement."

Her eyes widened. "My statement?"

"Relax, Ams. We need to know what you saw and when. You might know something in here—" he tapped her forehead with his index finger "—that you don't realize."

She nodded and moved toward the couch. Gathering a sleeping Carter in her arms, she thanked Nancy then faced Keith. "I suppose I can't get my clothes."

"No. I can't let you back into the room. I'll ask one of the deputies to get your things once they finish processing the scene."

Her shoulders sagged. "If you can grab the shopping bags, I'm ready."

The dark circles under her eyes and the tightness of her jaw worried him. His gut twisted into a knot. Absorbed in his humiliation, he hadn't contacted her over the past year, but she'd left a few voice mails and sent him texts on occasion. All unanswered by him. He felt like such a heel for ignoring her. Then three months ago, grief over his mother and Stacey had taken hold, and he hadn't noticed her silence. Maybe if he'd picked up on the signs, she wouldn't be running for her life. Just another mistake he'd add to his list of shining blunders.

He snatched the diaper bag and the sacks of supplies he'd collected from the hallway and guided her to his truck.

She buckled Carter into the car seat, still in the back seat from last night, and plopped into the passenger's side with a long sigh. "Let's go."

The events of the past few months hung like a weighted blanket over her. The vacant look in her eyes. The tension in her shoulders. Where had his fun-loving friend gone? The girl he'd crushed on since she'd beaned him in the head with a football at the age of twelve. He hadn't told her at the time. Because what self-respecting boy wanted the humiliation of a girl laughing at him? Why hadn't he confessed years later? He was an idiot. And now, he'd blown it. Hadn't he? His lips curved upward at the possibility. Stacey had been his friend, but Amy had taken on the title "girl of his dreams." Maybe once they found the killer, he'd sit down and have a heart-to-heart chat with her. And if she didn't kick him to the curb for his and Stacey's mistake, he'd take a chance and ask her out on a real date.

At the station, Keith secured the soft interview room for the duration of the day. Amy needed a place to relax and feel safe if he wanted her to answer his questions, and Carter deserved a room without noise and chaos.

Amy tossed a blanket on the floor. Placing the little man on his back, she handed him a rattle. "I can't thank you enough." She sunk into the plush gray leather couch. "I don't know what I'd do without you."

Keith lowered himself onto the matching easy chair and propped his ankle across his knee. "I'm always here for you, Ams. Even if we haven't talked in the past twelve months." He used to live for those phone calls and text messages. Even an email or two now and again, but after his and Stacey's world-class gaffe, he'd stepped away and hadn't noticed when Amy's attempts to contact him had stopped altogether. With his mother's passing and moving his father into his home, he'd allowed himself to believe she'd been too busy. What a lousy excuse. He should have accepted the fallout from his mistake and vowed to be a better friend to both Stacey and Amy. He hadn't wanted Amy to walk away from him, but he'd managed to mess that up too by turning his back on her.

Shaking off the self-recrimination, he tilted his head and studied her. Dark circles had formed under her eyes, and her entire body slumped. He picked up the pad of paper and a pen from the side table. "Wanna tell me what happened?"

She sighed. "I got up this morning and had a text from Trent. I was relieved to hear from him. He wanted to meet me at nine o'clock. Said he had news, so I responded to his text. I told him yes and gave him the name of the hotel and room number. It was only seven, and I realized I had to buy a few things for Carter, not to mention a few necessities for me. We kind of left Jackson in a hurry." Amy fiddled with the hem of her shirt.

Keith remained quiet in hopes she'd continue. His eyes drifted to Carter. The little boy had a firm grip on his giraffe rattle and shook it in the air. Why had Stacey kept a secret from him and her twin? Maybe Amy was wrong, and the person who'd killed Stacey hadn't made a mistake. Could it have been the father of her child? He shook his head, dislodging the far-fetched possibility. He studied the happy boy on the floor. Or was he... He shook his head. No. Stacey would have told him.

Amy returned her focus to him. "I grabbed the diaper bag, shoved my wallet inside and headed

to the pharmacy across the street from the hotel."
Her forehead creased. "I'd planned to drop off
my purchases and go to the hotel lobby for breakfast."

"But you walked into a mess?" He knew better than to put words in her mouth during a witness statement, but she looked so lost.

"The door was open a crack, so I looked in.
The room had been torn apart. That's when I
saw Trent." Amy wrapped her arms around her
waist and shivered. "There was so much blood."

Keith slipped from the chair and sat next to
her. He draped his arm around her and pulled
her close, tucking her under his chin. He laid
his cheek on her head and inhaled. The scent
of vanilla teased his senses—the same perfume
she'd worn as a teen. "I'm so sorry, Ams. No
one should ever have to see anything like that."

She sucked in a ragged breath. "I can't believe
he's gone."

Did Amy and this Trent guy have a relationship beyond him helping her? Keith closed his
eyes. He could dream all he wanted, but he
doubted Amy would welcome the idea of a relationship if she knew about his mistake with
her twin. Not Keith's finest moment, but what
made it worse was the fact he had never wanted
Stacey. He'd always wanted Amy. If Amy ever
found out what had happened, she'd put up a

barrier he'd never get through. Their friendship would be ruined. He refused to take that away. So much for the heart-to-heart he'd planned on having with her.

When Amy finished, he flicked the pen against his leg. "Why don't you take a break and take care of Carter while I get some work done? You can use this room for as long as you need today. Then we'll find a safe place for you to stay." Keith planned to talk with Sheriff Monroe about where Amy would stay while they investigated and found the person responsible for tormenting her.

"Thank you." She gripped his hand and squeezed. The sadness in her eyes tore his insides apart.

He stood, slipped from the room and headed to his office.

"Hey, man. Got the statement?" Kyle met him in the hallway.

Keith held out the notepad. "Want it in my wonderful handwriting, or would you like me to type it up?"

"You're kidding, right? I can't read that." Kyle's smile faded. "Get anything useful?"

"Not much." Keith gestured toward his office. "Come on in. Let's chat."

Detective Howard followed him in and plopped down in the chair opposite Keith's desk.

Jason glanced up from his side of the room. "What's up? You guys have something?" His partner scooted across the floor on his office chair.

Keith took his seat and tossed the notepad on the desk. Running his fingers through his hair, he leaned back and shared the information with his colleagues.

Kyle pitched in his take on what went down in the hotel room and the evidence discovered from Detective Jefferies's death. "I took the liberty and talked with Eagle Bay PD. They do have a record of a break-in at Ms. Baker's house. The place had been ransacked soon after Trent had hidden her. But no record of her original call."

Jason's brow arched. "So, what then—the guy is looking for something and just happens to leave bodies in his wake? I don't buy it."

"Neither do I. And I can't get past EBPD not contacting Anderson County Sheriff's Department." Kyle shook his head. "With a report of a murder on the cliff, the information to county should have been immediate."

Jason huffed. "What do you think is going on?"

"I'm not sure. But something's hinky with all this." Keith snapped his fingers. "Hang on. Since Ams is adamant that this is linked to Stacey's death, let's take another look." He swiveled his chair, dug through the file cabinet behind him and withdrew Stacey's file. He flipped through the cold case report and perused the document.

"Whoever shot her lit her car on fire. But the person responsible did a poor job. The fire department had it out before the whole thing went up." Keith tapped the paper. "Says here that Amy's camera was missing from the camera bag when Stacey's body was found. It could have been consumed in the fire, but Amy told me she popped the SD card and took it with her. I think it's more likely this guy wanted the pictures and took the camera. You know, retrieve the evidence against him and kill the only witness. But he goofed and killed the wrong twin, then found out the SD card wasn't there and is now after Amy."

"Seems like a sound theory. But then what? Trent got close to the truth?"

Keith nodded at his partner. "Makes about as much sense as anything, but the question remains—who? And who at EBPD is involved?"

They sat in silence, letting the theory sink in.

"So is this guy out to kill Amy or retrieve the proof of his crime?" Jason tapped his fingers on the arm of his chair.

"A crime which we don't even know happened."

Keith opened his mouth.

The man held up his hand. "I believe her, but

we don't have a body. We don't even have an investigation except for Trent's murder and Amy's road rage dude from yesterday."

"And don't forget whoever stopped the communication with ACSD." He had a hard time believing a cop was involved. But things like that happened from time to time.

"Sure would be nice to have those photos to corroborate her story." Jason sighed.

"She said she gave the SD card to Detective Jefferies. So unless it shows up in his things…" Keith shrugged and pinched the bridge of his nose. He knew what had to be done but didn't like the idea. "I'll take her to the cliff and check it out tomorrow."

Kyle nodded. "It's been three months, but hopefully, you'll find something to corroborate her story that we can use to open a full investigation." Kyle rubbed his eyes. "I wish we had a clue who this creep is."

"That makes two of us." A headache had gripped Keith's temples. Trouble had found his friend, and he had no clue how to stop it. One more thing to add to his guilt.

Jason rested his forearms on his knees. "I don't know about you guys, but we've got a whole lot of nothing when it comes to identifying the person responsible and their connection to EBPD. Not to mention the woman Amy saw fall over the cliff."

"We've got work to do. But my top priority is protecting Amy and baby Carter." Keith pushed to his feet. "I'm going to talk with the sheriff about her staying at my place with Dad and me. I'm hoping he'll agree to extra help monitoring the property until we catch this guy."

"I'll grab Doug and we'll continue investigating Trent's death while you deal with the other side of things." Kyle ambled to the exit and tapped his knuckles on the doorjamb. "Keep me in the loop."

Keith watched his friend walk out and turned to his partner. "What do you think, Jason? Want to be on protection duty for a few hours while I catch some shut-eye?" Keith grinned. He knew Jason spent all his extra time with his new wife, the department's forensic anthropologist and county coroner, Dr. Melanie Hutton-Cooper.

"Can I bring Mel with me?" His partner waggled his eyebrows.

"Oh, dude, you've got it bad."

"Yup. You'll get no argument from me on that one."

"Well, we all know she's a better shot than you, so sure." Keith figured Amy would like the female company, and another set of eyes never hurt.

"You wound me." Jason pulled the imaginary knife from his chest and pushed off the floor, rolling back to his desk.

Shaking his head at his partner's dramatics, Keith collected the files and grabbed his keys. "I'm heading to talk with Dennis, and then I'll get Amy and take her home." He glanced at his watch. "See you in a few hours?"

Already engrossed in a report, Jason waved without looking up. "Sounds like a plan."

Keith strode to Sheriff Monroe's office to fill him in and request the extra patrols. His mind whirled with the what-ifs. What if he'd been a better friend? What if Amy found out about his mistake with Stacey? And the big one—what if he couldn't figure out who was after Amy and Carter lost another mother? And Keith lost another friend.

THREE

Carter whined from the back seat of Keith's truck. Poor little guy, the long day had tuckered him out. Keith didn't blame the baby after spending hours at the sheriff's station. Carter needed a comfortable place to sleep, and the floor of the interview room wasn't it.

He glanced at Amy in the passenger seat. She looked ready to drop herself. The gash on her forehead had bruised, and fatigue shadowed her features. A shell of her former self, she rested her head on the window and gazed off into the distance.

Leaving her to her thoughts, he steered through town then pulled into his long drive. He parked in front of the farmhouse that he'd purchased five months ago, right before his mother died and his father came to live with him.

The old structure had required several updates but painting both the interior and exterior and repairing a few boards on the porch, along with installing new windows and doors, were the extent of the fixes. It hadn't taken long to make the place a home. The bonus being he had plenty of space for his dad and additional company. And maybe someday, a family.

"Let me grab the little guy for you." He dropped from the driver's side and scooted around the vehicle. After a fight with the five-point harness, the buckle released. "Come on, Carter, my man. How about we get you inside?"

Amy slid from her seat and pivoted to face him.

He handed the child off to her and grabbed the bags.

She took two steps and halted.

"What's wrong?" He went on high alert.

"Your house is amazing." She stood, staring at the dwelling.

"Thanks." His hand rested on her lower back, and his gaze shifted to the tree line. He didn't like her out in the open. Not until they had a better idea of what they were dealing with. "What do you say we head on in?" He led her up the steps and opened the front door. "Please, make yourself at home. I sent Dad to the store for groceries and a few more baby items."

"You didn't have to do that." Amy stepped into the living room and shifted to face him. Her pinched features and wariness returned. "But

I appreciate it and everything else you've done for us."

He hadn't been a good friend lately, but he planned to change that. He'd missed his childhood buddy. Dropping the bags to the floor, he wrapped her in a hug. She tensed beneath his touch, so he let go and took a step back. Her response to the friendly gesture meant to comfort her had awoken the realization of what he couldn't have. And for the better, since once Amy found out what he'd done, she'd never want more than a friendship from him, assuming she didn't walk away completely.

"That's what friends are for." Keith masked his disappointment and nodded toward the stairs. "I had one of the ladies from church stop by and set up a portable crib. It should be ready for little man's nap." He followed Amy up the stairs. "Second room on your right. Dad's is the first. I'm at the end of the hall on the left."

Amy opened the door and froze. "Keith. It's beautiful." She took a few steps into the room. "Is that one of your mom's quilts?" She ran her hand over the multicolored blanket with lavender flowers.

"It was her favorite. I had to keep it." He cleared the lump that had taken residence in his throat. "I'll put your things by the closet, and you're welcome to use the dresser. It's empty." He placed the bags in front of the closet door. "The rocking chair is—was—Mom's, too. It's pretty comfortable. Perfect for snuggling the little dude."

Amy placed a hand on his arm. "Thank you, Keith. I'm so grateful for all you've done." She jerked her hand away and bounced Carter on her hip, keeping her gaze anywhere but on Keith.

Her delicate touch shocked him. She'd always exuded strength. Her fragility puzzled him. When had she turned from the young girl from his youth to a gentle woman? He exhaled, disappointed by her reaction. Another reminder of the mistakes he'd made. "I know you must be tired. Why don't you two try to get some rest before dinner."

"Sounds like a wonderful idea. I'll fix Carter a bottle and see if he'll go down for a nap." She fumbled around in the diaper bag and pulled out a bottle with dried formula already measured out.

"Please, let me." Keith grabbed the plastic container and went to fill it with warm water. A few minutes later, he returned to find Carter's diaper changed and Amy in the rocking chair. The sight took Keith's breath away. His imagination got the best of him. What would it be like to have Amy holding their child? He shook his head to dislodge the errant thought. *Get it together, man. She deserves better than the likes of you.* "Here ya go."

"Thanks." She tested it on her wrist. "It's perfect."

Carter grabbed the bottle, and Amy helped him bring it to his mouth. The moment the baby started sucking, his eyes drooped closed. The long day at the station had taken its toll on the little guy.

"I'll leave you two. Come down after you get your own nap." Keith closed the door behind him. He made his way down the stairs and met his dad, Ian Young, coming from the kitchen. "Hey, Pops."

"Hey, yourself. Where's my sweet girl?"

"She's upstairs getting Carter down for a nap. You get everything?"

"Of course. I had a baby once a long time ago. Remember?" His dad chuckled. "Now, want to tell me what's going on with that girl?" Ian leaned against the doorjamb and crossed his arms over his chest.

Keith proceeded to give his father as many details as possible without overstepping the professional line. "So, you see, the theory is that Stacey was mistaken for Amy, and now Amy and Carter are in trouble."

"You know I'll help in any way I can." Ian rubbed the back of his neck. "Poor Stacey. Wonder what she was doing coming to Valley Springs that day."

"Beats me. Amy hadn't told her about witnessing a crime, so she wasn't coming for help. But that question does beg for an answer that might help untangle this mess." Too many seemingly unconnected parts somehow fit together, he was sure of it. But how? Keith moved to the door. "I'm going to check the perimeter. Whoever's after Amy seems determined. I don't want to let my guard down."

"Go. I'll put the supplies away while you take care of business." His father pushed from the wall and disappeared into the kitchen.

Keith stepped outside and scanned the area. He'd cleared the fallen limbs from the yard and added a fence line before he moved in. He wanted a dog but hadn't found the right one yet. But thanks to his planning ahead, he had a nice line of sight. No one could easily sneak up on the house without him or his father seeing them. The small shed on the back of the property could pose a problem. He'd ask Jason to bring a padlock to keep unwanted visitors out.

An hour later and after one final trip around the house, he shot up a prayer for Amy's safety and went inside.

"Everything okay out there?" His dad headed to his favorite brown leather recliner and plopped down.

Keith set the house alarm, kicked off his boots

by the back door then lowered himself onto the matching couch. He stretched out his legs under the coffee table and crossed his ankles. "For now. Let's keep the security system engaged at all times until this is over."

"Whatever you need to keep Amy and that little baby safe."

"Thanks." Keith laced his fingers over his chest and chatted with his father.

The stairs creaked. Keith pivoted and spotted Amy descending the staircase with a tiny bundle in her arms.

He rose and gestured to the couch. "I see the little man's awake. Did you get any rest?"

"Yes, thank you." Amy stopped next to the armrest. "Mr. Young, it's good to see you again."

"You, too. And it's Ian, please." Keith's father scooted to the edge of his seat. "May I see that baby I've heard about?"

"Certainly." Amy strode over and laid Carter in Ian's outstretched arms. "He'll be complaining about an empty tummy soon. I don't think that kid is ever full. I'll go heat up a bottle." She headed to the kitchen.

Ian's eyes never left the baby as he settled back into his chair. "So, you're Carter. Well, aren't you a cutie?"

Keith smiled as he watched his father coo and

baby talk with the infant. The man was certainly enjoying himself.

Bottle in hand, Amy waltzed over to Ian. "Would you like to feed him?"

"Sure would." Keith's father beamed.

Amy handed the man the bottle and a burp cloth then took a seat opposite Keith on the sofa.

"I haven't done this in years. But I don't think you ever lose the knack." Ian held the bottle to Carter's mouth.

Sucking and slurping filled the otherwise silent room.

Amy chuckled. "He's always been a noisy eater."

"Just like his father." Ian kissed the top of Carter's head.

Keith exchanged glances with Amy then narrowed his gaze on his father. "Excuse me?"

"Why didn't you tell me I have a grandson?" The older man's attention never wavered from the little guy in his arms.

"What are you talking about?" Keith's mind spun. According to Amy, her twin hadn't told anyone the father's name. Although he had to admit, the timing was right.

Ian's eyebrows rose. "You're trying to tell me you didn't know Carter is yours? He looks just like you did as a babe. The only difference, he has his momma's eyes."

Keith opened his mouth to speak, but Amy stepped in. "Stacey didn't tell anyone who the father is." She pivoted to face him, eyes wide. "Is it possible?"

Heat rushed up Keith's neck and face. He'd hoped to go to his grave with his secret, but that wasn't going to happen. Not now. He swallowed the golf ball–size lump in his throat. Not knowing what to say, he simply nodded.

She gasped. "Why didn't you tell— Why didn't she tell— How come—"

"I'm sorry, Ams." He reached for her but changed his mind.

Fire lit behind her eyes. "How could you?"

"It was a mistake. One night, that's all. Stace and I agreed to never talk about it."

She bolted from the couch and spun to face him. "One night?" Her voice skyrocketed. "My sister was a one-night stand?"

"I didn't mean it that way." Keith glanced at his dad, who tried hard to appear like he wasn't listening. But how could he not hear the horrible thing his son had done?

Amy's fist clenched. "How *did* you mean it?"

"It was stupid on both our parts. We had celebrated Stacey's promotion, and one thing led to another. It's not something I'm proud of."

Amy's eyes narrowed, and she clenched her teeth.

His father cleared his throat. "I…um…am sorry. This spat is my fault. I shouldn't have said anything."

Keith scrubbed his hands down his face. "No, Dad. It's good that it's finally out in the open." He prayed Amy would accept his apology and continue to let him protect her—and his possible son.

Carter against his chest, Ian patted the boy's back and rocked back and forth. "Is there any way to find out besides a paternity test?"

Amy shook her head. "I'm afraid that secret died with her…unless—"

Keith froze. "What?"

"The envelope! It's from Stacey." Amy raced up the stairs.

Keith scooted to the edge of his seat. He wanted to hurry after her, yet he didn't want to at the same time. Would whatever they found change his life forever? Had Stacey told Amy the truth within that golden packet? Was he Carter's father? Did he want to be? So many questions whirled in his head.

"Not your finest moment, son." His dad interrupted his thoughts with more of a statement than an admonishment.

"Yeah, I know. Something I'll regret for the rest of my life." Keith stood. "I should join her."

He motioned toward the baby in his father's arms. "You good?"

"Of course. My grandson and I need time to get to know each other."

"Dad." If the man kept this up without proof, the rumors would fly around town. Then again, what if his father was right?

"No sense denying the truth. This little guy is your mini-me with deep blue eyes. But go. See if Stacey's last words will put your mind at rest."

Keith nodded and followed Amy's path up the stairs.

Time to man up and accept the truth, whatever that might be.

Amy flung open the door and marched into her temporary bedroom. She paused in front of the nightstand. The envelope in question resided in the top drawer, taunting her to remove what Stacey had left inside. Too tired to deal with it when they arrived a few hours ago, she'd stuffed it in the nightstand and fallen onto the bed. Amy wasn't sure what she wanted to find. Stacey's reasons why she hadn't confided in her? Confirmation that Keith was Carter's father? An explanation as to why her sister had kept it a secret? All of the above?

If she could, Amy would strangle her twin right about now. Not to mention what she wanted to do to Keith. How could they? A piece of her heart broke off and fluttered to the ground. Her dream of someday with Keith floated away. He had wanted Amy's twin and not her; once again, she came in second to her sister.

"Ams?" His hand rested on her shoulder.

She shrugged it off and spun to face him. "Don't."

He held his hands up in surrender. "I'm not sure if Carter's mine, but I'd like to explain what happened."

"What happened? I *know* what happened."

"Ams. Please, listen."

She exhaled and nodded. Might as well get the painful truth out in the open.

His fingers burrowed through his hair. "After you took off the night we celebrated Stace's promotion, the waitress came by with a bottle of champagne. Said the owner wanted to thank Stacey for her service and congratulate her on her promotion. We accepted, and that was the start of a series of bad choices."

"No kidding." She folded her arms across her chest. The betrayal hurt. Her twin and her best friend had stabbed her in the back.

He ignored her snark and continued. "The next day, I called her and apologized for my lapse in judgment. She hadn't blamed me and accepted her own role in our moment of stupidity. But our friendship never truly recovered." His hangdog face spoke to his regret.

Still not ready to forgive him, but she had to agree. "I suppose not." At least the man acknowledged responsibility for his actions.

"Look, Ams. I'm a different man now."

"You always had such a high moral compass." Her shoulder hitched. "I guess that's why this is such a shock." That and the fact he had wanted Stacey and not her. That stung more than anything.

"That might be true, but now I have a faith to back it up."

She stared at him as if he'd grown another head. "You believe in God?"

A small smile pulled at the corner of his mouth. "Better yet, He has my heart."

Of all the things she'd imagined about this man, that had never been one of them.

"I'm sorry, Ams. I not only disrespected your sister, but I hurt you, too. I hope someday you can forgive me."

She shook her head. Forgiveness was a long way off, but her heart tugged at her. Why had she taken this so personally? He and Stacey had been consenting adults. But Amy knew why. She'd had a crush on Keith since they were kids. And now, to find out he'd chosen her sister over her...

She sighed. It wasn't his fault he wanted Stace and not her. Story of her life. "Maybe, someday."

Pain flickered in his eyes. "Guess a maybe is better than nothing. Should we see what Stace had to say?"

Amy pulled open the drawer and withdrew the large envelope. Time to find out what her twin had decided to reveal. Bending the tabs, she opened the flap and peered inside. Two pieces of paper waited for her. Amy pulled them out.

"Well?"

She looked at one page and then the next. "A letter and Carter's birth certificate."

"I assumed you already had his birth certificate." Keith peered over her shoulder. "What does it say?"

Holding it out so they both could read it, she glanced at the sticky note on the document. "Says she changed her mind and updated his birth certificate before she left on deployment." Her hands shook as she read. "Carter Ian Young." The breath whooshed from her lungs. "Mother, Stacey Marie Baker, and Father, Keith Thomas Young. Guess that answers that." Amy pivoted to see his reaction.

Keith's face turned sugar white. "I'm his father?" he whispered.

How could she lash out in anger when his world had flipped on its side? Oh, she was mad, but the man looked as if he might pass out.

She clutched his arm. "Breathe, Keith."

"I mean, when Dad said Carter looked just like me, I knew it was possible, but I never expected it to be true."

She handed the document to Keith and waited, allowing him time to process the new information.

A tear trickled down his cheek. She reached up and swiped it away with her thumb.

His eyes met hers. "I'm a dad."

Her heart twisted. For herself and for Keith. "Yes, you are."

He staggered to the bed and lowered himself to the mattress. Sitting on the edge, he ran a hand over his face. "What does the letter say?"

She sat beside him and focused on her sister's handwriting.

Dear Amy,

I guess since you are reading this, I didn't make it home from deployment. I'm sorry for leaving you alone in this world, but God had other plans for me. Thank you for taking care of Carter. I'm sorry you had to bear the weight of my poor judgment. I love Carter with all my heart, and I'm thankful you agreed to be his legal guardian and always be there for him.

"What does she mean by that?" Keith pointed to the part about the legal guardian.

"Her job in the Army required her to have someone take legal custody of Carter in case something happened to her while on duty. Since she wouldn't name the father at the time, for all intents and purposes, I became Carter's legal parent."

"I still don't understand why she didn't tell me."

Amy had no words. She didn't understand either. She continued with the letter.

I hope I did the right thing, but in case I chickened out before I left on deployment, there's something you need to know. Keith is Carter's father. I'm sorry I didn't tell you sooner, but I knew you'd be disappointed in me.

Please let Keith know that it was nothing against him. I was ashamed and had hoped to keep him from the same. I hope he's not too mad at me. Keith and I might have made a huge mistake, but I'll never be sorry for the beautiful baby we created.

I know you'll do the right thing, Ams. Raise Carter as your own, and please, someday, when you feel the time is right, let Carter know his father.

I love you, sis.

Stacey

Tears burned as Amy reread her sister's words. Stacey had never made it to that deployment after the birth of her son. She'd died on her final day of leave.

"Do you think that's why she was heading to Valley Springs that day? To tell me about Carter?" Keith whispered.

"I think it's a real possibility."

"Oh, Ams—" Keith's phone buzzed. He pulled it out of his pocket and glanced at the screen. "Hold on." He answered the call. "Hey, Jason."

Amy felt his body tense. She shifted to look at him.

"Okay. Will do. Thanks for letting me know." With that, he hung up.

"News?"

He nodded. "They found an email in Trent's inbox from the Valley Springs chief of police, asking Trent to meet him at your hotel room early this morning."

"The chief of police? He's the killer?" Amy's heart pounded. First the shock of her sister and Keith's betrayal, now this.

"Jason doesn't think so. Someone hacked the chief's email. But he wants us at the sheriff's station first thing tomorrow morning to go over the new information." Keith stood and turned serious. "Are you okay with me protecting you, or would you like me to request someone else?"

Was she? She might be angry at Keith, but there was no one she wanted more to keep them safe. If only she could fully trust him. But now that he was protecting his son, maybe he wouldn't let her down this time.

FOUR

Keith stood in the doorway of Sheriff Dennis Monroe's office. "You wanted to see us, Sheriff?"

"Come on in." Dennis motioned to the two chairs in front of his desk. He shook Amy's hand. "Nice to meet you, and please accept my condolences for your sister."

"Thank you." She sat, spine straight, and rested her hands in her lap. Tears teetered on her lashes.

The tension radiating from her made Keith jumpy. He'd like to pull her into a hug and comfort her, but that wasn't a good idea. The strain between them had been as tight as a stretched rubber band. He'd tiptoed around her this morning, not wanting to do anything to upset her any more than Stacey's announcement already had. A year ago, the hesitation wouldn't have existed. But now, he'd lost one of his best friends, become a father and hurt the woman beside him.

He cleared the emotion from his throat. "What can we do for you?"

Sheriff Monroe leaned forward in his chair. He rested his elbows on his desk and steepled his fingers. "I wanted to keep Ms. Baker in the loop and see if she had remembered anything else that might help us find the person who's after her."

"I'm sorry, but I don't know how I can help. I've told you everything I know." Amy squeezed her hands so tight her fingers turned white.

The sheriff pinched his lips together, and the crease between his brows deepened. "What about the death of Detective Jefferies? Do you have anything else to add to your statement?"

"No. Sorry." Amy's eyes widened. "Wait. You think I killed him?"

Keith held his breath, waiting for Monroe's response. He knew Amy was innocent, but the team had to do their job. He had to keep his mouth shut or be pushed out of the investigation altogether.

"Not at all. In fact, I heard from Kyle this morning. Video footage from the hotel and the businesses next door and across the street confirm Jefferies entered your room after you left and the killer entered right behind him. However, the man knew what he was doing. We don't have a clear view of the suspect's face. All we have are a general height and weight. But those events, along with the time you returned to the hotel and ran into Detective Young, clear Amy as a suspect."

"Thanks for the quick turnaround." Keith released the pent-up breath.

She brought a trembling hand to her mouth. "Yes, thank you."

"My pleasure." Dennis gave Amy a reassuring smile then turned his attention to Keith. "Kyle will continue with the investigation into Jefferies's death. I want you to focus on Amy and the threat against her and her twin's murder. Since we believe there's a good chance the three are related, work closely with Kyle and share information."

"Will do. We really need that SD card with the photos." He glanced at Amy. "Do you have any idea what Trent did with it?"

Her eyes drifted to the floor. "No."

"I'll have Kyle search for it." Keith gripped the arms of his chair, braced himself for the fallout of his next suggestion. "Since we don't have the pictures to confirm what Amy saw, I think it's time to take Amy to revisit the cliff." He waited for Amy to respond.

She sat motionless.

His gaze connected with his boss's.

Dennis's eyebrow rose.

"Ams?"

"We wouldn't ask if it wasn't important," the sheriff chimed in.

Her face had lost all color. The trauma from her experience had hit her harder than he'd originally thought. He laid his hand on top of hers. "I know you don't want to, but I believe it's the only way to figure this out. You might remember something small that will help. Think about Carter."

Amy straightened her shoulders and yanked her hand away. She pinned Keith with a glare. "Carter deserves to have peace in his life. I'll do it—for *him*."

Ouch. That hurt. Her words hit their mark. He'd hurt his best friend in the worst possible way. Amy had good reason to be angry, and now he'd asked her to relive witnessing a murder. Regret and guilt filled him. "Of course." Keith eased himself from the seat and focused on the sheriff. "We'll head out then. I'll let you know if we get anything new."

"Sounds good." Dennis stepped around his desk. "I appreciate this, Ms. Baker."

Amy nodded and headed out the door without Keith.

"Sorry, man." His boss and friend slapped him on the shoulder. "I think I hit a beehive with a stick."

"It's okay. She's tough." Keith hoped with everything in him that he hadn't lied to Dennis. "Talk to you in a couple of hours." Keith exhaled and left the office to find Amy.

God, I could use Your wisdom here. How do I handle all this?

Every bruise and sore muscle chose that moment to throb. Amy's nerves sparked like live wires, and her head pounded. She burst through the station door and sucked in a lungful of fresh air. She closed her eyes and lifted her face to the midmorning sun. Birds chirped from their perch in the trees, and the aroma from the diner drifted in her direction. All normal occurrences, in stark contrast to her out-of-control life.

Times like these, she missed her sister. Her confidante, or so she'd thought. Tears burned behind her eyes. *Why, Stace?*

Amy knew in her heart that her twin hadn't set out to hurt her, and if she were honest with herself, neither had Keith.

Taking several deep breaths, she pushed aside her resentment the best she could. Stacey deserved justice, and the killer she'd witnessed deserved to be behind bars.

Hands rested on her shoulders. "I'm sorry we have to do this."

The desire to lean into him overwhelmed her. He'd hurt her—badly. She fought her conflicting feelings and accepted his support but didn't give in to his comfort. "I don't want to, but that's not an option."

"I'd love to shield you from revisiting the cliff. But I—"

"That won't solve the case."

"No. It won't." His hands tightened then he moved her to face him. "I am truly sorry—for everything."

"I know you are. I'm just not sure I can let it go."

"I understand."

Did he? Did he understand that he'd crushed her by sleeping with her twin? By hiding from her? By choosing Stacey over her? And that's where the problem lay. Keith's choice in twins. But that was her problem, not his. One she'd have to work through on her own.

Amy stepped toward his truck. "Let's get going and get this over with. I want to get back to Carter as soon as possible." She trusted Ian to take care of his grandson, but that wasn't the point. She wanted to be with him.

She felt Keith's gaze on her back, but she refused to look at him. If she did, the tears pushing on her eyes might find their way to her cheeks.

Keith unlocked the doors, and Amy slid into the passenger seat. Dread swirled in her belly.

What if the killer followed them to the cliff and repeated his actions from three months ago?

The engine rumbled over the silence lingering in the cab of Keith's truck. The hum of the tires, a welcome white noise, filled the awkwardness between him and Amy. She had said little since their departure from the sheriff's station, leaving him with his own thoughts. The recent events tumbled in his mind and landed on Carter. He'd thought someday he'd have a family, but he'd never thought it would be like this. Why hadn't Stacey told him? He would have been there for her. Hadn't she known that? Shock continued to mask the simmering anger of missing out on the first four months of his son's life. He rolled his fisted grip over the leather steering wheel. Four months he'd never get back. Why had Stacey kept such a secret?

"You doing okay over there?" Amy's voice pulled him from his musing.

"I could ask you the same thing." It had to be a jolt for her. It was obvious Stacey never planned to tell Amy of their one night together. And to find out he'd betrayed Amy's trust—he shook his head.

She shrugged. "I became Carter's legal guardian four months ago, soon after he was born. I've had time to adjust, but you, on the other hand, just found out you have a son. My twin sister's *son*." He didn't miss the bite in her tone.

He'd hurt Amy by his actions, and he had to somehow make things right. Tall order. "I'd be lying if I said I had it all worked out in my head."

"I get that." Amy picked at her fingernails.

The cool air flowed from the vents, not only cooling the interior of the truck but his frustration. Amy had thrown him a limb to grasp onto by starting the line of communication. He'd like to keep it going, but they'd soon be at the trailhead that led to the cliff, and he had to concentrate on the task at hand. "Listen, I know we have a lot to talk through."

"You can say that again." Hurt lined her words.

"I can't say I'm ready to ignore the proverbial elephant in the room, but we have to focus on your safety and Carter's. I can apologize until I'm hoarse, but I'm not sure that will make a difference right now."

"Probably not." She exhaled and shifted, putting her back to him, and looked out the window. "You're right. We were friends long before all this happened. Let's put it aside for a later conversation."

He breathed a sigh of relief. "I can if you can. I'd rather put my efforts into keeping you safe and finding out who's after you."

"What's your opinion of this guy?"

Ooo-kay. His mind struggled to shift gears with the quick change in topic. Green trees whizzed by as he drove down the quiet two-lane highway. Giving himself a moment, he adjusted the vents and turned up the air-conditioning in the truck to counter the rising temperature outside. "He obviously wants something."

"True. When he killed Stacey, my camera went missing. I'm guessing he took it and wanted the SD card with the pictures."

He glanced at her then returned his focus to the road. The report stated that an empty camera bag had been tossed aside, and he and Jason had already assumed the fact had a significant meaning. "It would sure be nice if you still had the memory card."

She bit her lower lip and refused to look in his direction.

Keith drummed the steering wheel. The woman had his brain scrambling in multiple directions. Between the attempt on Amy's life and news of his son, his patience had worn thin. "What aren't you telling me?" he groused.

She shook her head and slid a glance in his direction. "Like I told you, Detective Jefferies had the SD card, so look there."

"According to Kyle, someone trashed Trent's house and car. If this guy found the photos, we can make an educated guess that your attacker has what he's looking for. He has no reason to search your things anymore."

Her eyes widened. "I get the feeling you aren't going to tell me he'll leave me alone."

He wished that were the case, but the chances were slim. "No. Not if he thinks you can identify him."

"I was afraid you were going to say that." She slouched in her seat. Nibbling on her fingernail, she stared out the passenger-side window.

"Can you?" Keith's eyes drifted to the rear-view mirror to confirm they hadn't picked up a tail. His shoulders relaxed when he determined no one had followed them from the sheriff's station.

"Can I what?"

"Identify him?"

"If I could, we wouldn't be in the middle of this nightmare," she snipped.

He had nothing to be sorry for. He needed the confirmation, but he might as well play nice. "Of course. Sorry."

Trees towered over the road on his left, and a steep rocky bank overlooking the swift-running river loomed on his right. He loved this area of the county, but the curves in the road made for interesting driving during the winter months when snow and ice covered the county highway. However, with the summer sun shining down, the water sparkled, and light arrowed its glow through the leaves on the trees. The area had a serene beauty about it. He resisted the urge to roll down his window and allow the scent of the trees to waft in, letting him remember his grandma hanging clothes on the line in her backyard.

A smile tugged on his lips at the memory. He tapped his brakes as he approached the curve.

Nothing happened.

Pushing harder on the pedal, his foot went to the floor. He gripped the steering wheel tighter. "Um, Ams, we have a problem."

She spun to face him. "What is it?"

"The brakes are gone." He tried the hopeless action one more time. Still nothing. "Call 9-1-1. Tell them an officer needs assistance and give them our location."

Amy fumbled with her phone and placed the call. "Okay, now what?"

The fear in her voice rattled him, but he had to keep his attention on the task at hand. He couldn't leave Carter an orphan after he'd just found him.

Amy sat up straight and gripped the dashboard. "Can we make it to the straightaway?"

"Not sure. It's still a couple miles from here." His gaze flew to the rearview mirror and landed on the empty car seat. Keith sent up a thanks to God that they'd left Carter home with his dad.

The air whooshed from Keith's lungs at the sight of a large deer carcass in the middle of his path. The tree-lined side of the road held less room than the riverside. But without the ability to slow, could he make it past?

"Hold on, Ams." The loose gravel from the tiny shoulder of the road spit from his tires, pulling his vehicle toward the drop-off. He fought for control. The tires held, then slipped too far for him to recover.

"Hold on!" Keith flung his arm in front of Amy in a futile attempt to stop her from whipping forward.

The truck slid on the rocks and careened over the edge.

Amy's scream pierced the air.

Plunging nose-first into the swift-moving river below, the front end hit the water with a bone-jarring jolt.

The airbags deployed, and silence descended.

Keith lifted his head from the deflating airbag. White powder tickled his nose and left a chalk taste in his mouth. He sputtered and did his best to wipe the offending substance away.

His face had taken the brunt of the impact, but his left shoulder screamed at him. It took him a few moments to piece together what had happened. Amy.

"Amy. You okay?" He strained to see her face.

With the engine down and the truck's bed up, the odd angle made it difficult to sit upright.

A moan emanated from the passenger seat.

His feet felt cold and damp. The trickle of water caught his attention. He blinked. The realization that water was seeping into the cab had his senses on high alert. He had to get the windows open before the engine sank below the waterline. *Please don't let the electric controls be dead yet.* The attempt to lift his left arm sent a flash of lightning zipping across his vision. He sucked in air, taming the nausea churning in his belly. He reached across with his right hand and punched the buttons to lower the glass. The window motor whined but hadn't given out. So far. Two inches from the bottom, the mechanism stopped. *Thank You, Lord.* It might not have made it all the way down before shorting out, but they had enough room to escape.

"Come on, Ams. We have to get out of here." He shook her arm.

"Keith?" She rolled her head to face him.

He pushed the white bag with his right hand, releasing more of the chalky substance into the air. "Can you move?"

"I think so."

"Unbuckle and climb out the window and onto the top of the cab."

Amy fumbled for her seat belt. "What about you?"

"I'll be right behind you." He hoped. He reached out with his right arm and helped her with her seat belt. Amy slipped out the opening. Her feet disappeared from sight.

Keith exhaled. Now to extract himself.

He fumbled with the seat belt lock, but it refused to budge. His left arm was practically useless—a dislocated shoulder would be his guess.

Water had risen to his upper thigh. Time was running out. He had to get Amy to the shore before either one of them drowned, and Carter lost both parents.

Carter. His son.

God, I want to be around to raise my boy. Please help me get free. If that's not in Your plans, protect Amy. Carter needs one of us.

"What's taking so long? You have to get out. Now!"

He glanced to his left. Amy's upside-down face came into view.

"Can't get my belt undone." Water had hit his waist and was rising fast.

"Knife," Amy demanded.

"What?"

"You're a creature of habit. Pocketknife. Right pants pocket. Hurry."

How had he forgotten that? Maybe he hit his head harder than he thought. He shifted, and stars burst behind his eyelids. The pain from his left shoulder had him gasping for air. His stomach roiled, but he had no time to waste. He swallowed down the bile and retracted his knife.

"Give it." Amy held out her hand.

He obliged and watched as she hung through the window and cut the thick material. "Can you get out on your own?"

"I think so." He grabbed the door frame and pulled himself through the opening. He plunked down on the top of the cab next to Amy, and she slapped the knife into his hand. "Thanks for the save."

Now what was he going to do? With his shoulder out of place, he couldn't swim her to the riverbank, even though only twenty feet spanned the distance. Staying wasn't an option either.

Okay, God, now what?

Amy cringed at the pain flashing through Keith's eyes. His shoulder sat at an odd angle.

The river water had risen to the top of the hood and crept toward the roof at a terrifying rate. Within minutes the truck would be fully submerged. She knew Keith's silence meant he was thinking—plotting—a way to the shoreline.

It might be summer, but the cool water made her shiver. Not cold enough to kill, but if they survived the current and made it to the bank, they'd be chilled to the bone. She had to do something.

Mind made up, she pivoted to face Keith. His pallor worried her, but she didn't have time to focus on anything except getting them out of the river. "Okay, so here's the deal. You're in no shape to swim. Lower yourself into the water before the truck sinks and hold on. I'll get behind you and swim us out."

He shook his head. "Not happening. I'm too heavy, and the current's too swift. You won't make it."

She cupped his cheeks and got in his face. "Listen here, mister. We are out of options. There's no way you can swim with that arm. Now get in the water before we both go under."

The internal fight he had with himself was visible, but he acquiesced. "All right, you win. But if it's between saving yourself or both of us drowning, leave me behind. Carter needs you."

The man's willingness to sacrifice himself for her and his son twisted her heart. No, not her. Just his son. The thought physically hurt. But she couldn't blame him for making his son a priority.

No matter how much it pained her that Keith had chosen Stacey, Carter came first. She put her pettiness aside. Swallowing hard, Amy steeled her resolve to get them both out alive. It would be tricky with his weight and the strong current, but she could do this—had to do this. She had to make sure they both survived. "He needs his father too, so get moving."

Keith held on to the door frame and slid down into the river. The truck jerked, and water bubbled around him. He looked up at her. "Hurry up. This thing is going down fast."

It was now or never. She mimicked his actions. The cold water stole her breath. She gasped, then pushed the discomfort away. She maneuvered behind him. She had no choice but to loop her arm under his damaged one and around his chest. "I've got you. Whatever happens, don't fight me. Got it?"

He moaned at the movement. "Got it," he said through gritted teeth.

She took his weight and released her hold of the metal frame. "Here we go." The river pulled her along at a rapid rate. Amy had to think fast. She wasn't strong enough to swim against the current. Maybe without Keith in tow, but as things were, she only had one option. Instead of fighting the current, she allowed it to take them a few more yards down the river before she gradually steered them toward land. "I'm going to slowly veer us toward the bank." Her struggle eased when Keith helped with his own kicks.

"Ams, you okay?"

"Can't talk. Have to focus." She needed all her strength and concentration to get them to land.

A branch stuck out in front of her. She pivoted to shield Keith from the piece of wood. It struck her back and sent her off at an angle. Her back burned from the abrupt contact, but the redirection helped her path to the river's edge.

"Please. Let me go. Carter needs you."

"Not happening." Amy firmed up her grip and made her angle to the bank sharper. Several hard kicks later, her heel struck the riverbed. She grunted. Her leg throbbed at the sudden jolt. Amy disentangled herself from Keith and stood. She grabbed his collar and pulled. The newest bruise on her back protested the movement. She stumbled and went down on her knees.

"I've got you." He rolled over, struggled to his feet and pulled her up. Once on solid ground, he collapsed onto his back.

Amy dropped to the solid surface, facing the sky. Her breaths came in heavy pants. The rescue had taken a lot out of her. Good thing they hadn't gone in far from the water's edge, not to mention the diversion from the stray branch, or they never would have made it. "Thanks for helping. I couldn't have done it without you kicking with me."

His hand found hers and squeezed. "I forgot you were a lifeguard and varsity swimmer in high school. Thanks for the save."

"I'd say anytime, but I'd be lying." She rolled her head to the side and smiled at him.

A throaty chuckle joined sirens, filling the air. The cavalry had arrived.

"Keith! Amy!" Jason's voice filtered from above.

"Yeah, we're here," Keith yelled back.

Pebbles and dirt tumbled down the embankment ahead of Jason. "Thought you'd go for a swim today?" Keith's partner gave them a toothy grin.

"Very funny. Ethan and Brent close by?" Keith closed his eyes. His face contorted in pain.

"What's wrong?" Jason's tone turned serious.

Amy sat up and pointed to Keith's arm. "I think he has a dislocated shoulder."

"Think? I'm pretty sure it's not supposed to dip that way." Jason shook his head and lifted his radio. "Ethan, we need some assistance."

"Coming down." The paramedic's voice emanated from the radio.

"Want to tell me how you ended up in the river?" Jason squatted next to them.

Keith's gaze drilled into her. "My guess, Amy's tormentor is more determined than ever to eliminate her."

Her throat went dry, and the world spun around her. The man who'd run her off the road and ransacked her hotel room had proved he was still capable of murder after killing Stacey and leaving Detective Jefferies dead for Amy to find. Now he had her in his deadly sights. Amy knew the why, but the who eluded her.

Could Keith and his partner protect her, or would she end up dead like her twin sister?

FIVE

Happy to be out of the hospital but grumpy with the sling, Keith held the sheriff's station's door open for Amy. The doctor had put his shoulder back in place, wrapped it tightly with tape and sent him home to rest. Keith wanted nothing more than to go back to his house and get to know his son, maybe even take a nap, but Sheriff Monroe had requested a visit from him and Amy as soon as the doc released them.

"Thanks." Amy ambled through the door, her movements stiff, like she'd run a marathon. Keith assumed that's what she felt like after dragging him through the rushing water. The little effort he'd used to help had his leg muscles burning, and she'd done most of the work.

The necessity of her actions grated on him. He was supposed to protect her, not have her rescuing him. But that was what had happened. She'd saved his bacon and pulled off an incredible feat. How could he not be grateful? He stuffed his man pride down and followed her through the entrance.

Placing his free hand on her lower back, he guided her through the station to Sheriff Dennis Monroe's office.

Before Keith could knock, Dennis bellowed, "Come in."

Keith ushered Amy to one of the chairs and sank into the other. Finding the soft leather a bit too comfortable, he fought off the effects of the pain meds the doc had given him.

Jason had parked the car and then joined them a couple minutes later. His partner stood, leaning against the wall with his arms crossed, looking none too happy about the turn of events.

Monroe peered over the top of his steepled fingers. "How's the shoulder, Young?"

"Sore, but I'll live. Doc said to be careful since the muscles are weak." Keith adjusted the sling in an attempt to ease the pressure on his injured arm. "But he taped it up good and tight. Guess he knows me."

Monroe rolled his eyes. "Probably a good assumption after your sprained knee fiasco. And you, Ms. Baker?"

"Amy. Please." She toyed with the hem of the borrowed ACSD T-shirt Jason had supplied her with at the hospital to replace her soaked clothes.

"Amy then."

"I'm fine. A little shook up, and tomorrow I'll be wishing I'd worked out more, but all in all, I'm okay."

"Good. Glad to hear it."

Keith watched as Amy's gaze drifted around the room.

"You gave Jason your statement, but I wanted to see if there's anything I can do for you. Amy, I know you have a son, and keeping you and your child safe is my top priority." He motioned to Keith and Jason. "Our priority. I've asked Jason to stand guard at Keith's while the two of you get some much-needed rest."

The mention of Carter stole the air from the room. Amy's son. His son. His boss didn't know. For that matter, neither did his partner. Keith hadn't had the opportunity to disclose the new information. He'd better rectify that issue, and the sooner, the better. That was going to be interesting. Might as well get it over with.

Keith spoke up. "Sir, there's something you need—"

Amy gasped.

"What's wrong?" Keith shifted and took Amy's hand. A gesture that he'd done a lot lately.

Eyes focused on a photo on the wall, Amy stood and walked over to the picture. "Who are these people?"

Dennis rounded his desk and joined her.

"That's a picture from the last election. From left to right, me, Mayor Nolan Taylor and his assistant Debbie Ackers." He pointed to the people in the background. "And that's Jason and the mayor's wife, Sheila."

Keith moved next to her. "What is it?"

Amy's lower lip quivered.

"Ams?"

"That young woman." She tapped the glass of the frame. "You said her name was Debbie?" Amy hugged her middle. "She's the one I saw shot and fall over the cliff."

"The mayor's assistant? Are you sure?" The news stunned Keith. Although come to think about it, he hadn't seen Debbie in quite a while.

She nodded. "I have proof."

"You what?" Keith spun her to face him. "I thought you gave it to Detective Jefferies."

"I did, but I kept a copy. I had a gut feeling I might need it."

Keith pinched the bridge of his nose. Of all the things to keep secret. "You lied to me."

"No, I didn't. I said that I gave Trent *the* SD card. I didn't say I gave him the *only* SD card. I made a copy for security's sake."

"Semantics." She couldn't be serious with that argument.

Amy glared at him. "I was supposed to what? Put all my trust in you after a year of not hearing from you? After finding out that Carter's your son?" She yanked out of his hold. "You were my friend, my best friend. Then I find out you and my twin sister…" Tears flooded her eyes. "If you'll excuse me." Amy fled from the room, leaving Keith standing alone with his boss and partner.

Jason cleared his throat. "Sorry, man."

"Yeah, well, can't say she's wrong." Keith rubbed his forehead. "I really messed things up."

Dennis moved next to him, squeezed his good shoulder and grinned. "I guess congratulations are in order, Dad."

Yes, he was now a dad, and it felt pretty good. "Thanks."

"I have a feeling there's a story behind all this, but just know we're here for you and your son. Not to mention Amy." Jason headed for the door. "I'll get patrols assigned and call Melanie. We'll take the first shift. You and Amy need some rest, and I surmise you need time with Carter."

"I appreciate that. I'll fill you in later on the details, but you're right, I haven't had much opportunity to spend time with him." The pain in Keith's arm reappeared. He cradled his sling and released a long breath. The weight of the recent events and his near-death experience pressed down on him. His body craved time to recuperate. "Rest sounds like a great idea." He turned to Monroe. "Anything else, Sheriff?"

Dennis chuckled at his all-business mode. "That'll be all. And Jason, sign me up for a shift."

"You got it, boss." Jason saluted and held the door open for Keith.

Walking down the hall in search of Amy, Keith turned to his partner. "I wasn't keeping a secret."

"It's okay. I don't expect you to tell me everything...but a kid is kinda big."

"You don't understand. Amy's sister didn't tell anyone who the father was. Including me. I just found out."

"That's a tough one, man." Jason blew out a breath. "Let us know if we can do anything."

"Will do." Keith spotted Amy sitting at his desk. "Better go lick my wounds, then try to patch things up with Ams."

He and Amy had a lot to discuss. And on the top of the list was where to find the SD card she'd hidden. He prayed they found evidence on the images because, if not, he might lose her to the madman for good.

The silent drive to Keith's put Amy on edge. He'd escorted her out of the station to the rental truck Jason arranged while they'd been at the hospital then clammed up.

Anger and a bit of humiliation swirled inside

her. When they arrived at the house, Ian had Carter napping in the living room, so she escaped upstairs, unwilling to face Keith after her explosion in the sheriff's office. She flopped on the bed and tossed and turned for the next couple of hours. She awoke a short time later, heart racing and gasping for breath. The horrible nightmares of water, gunshots and cliffs had plagued her dreams. Pulse rate back to normal, she lay staring at the ceiling, guilt tugging at her heart. She'd really lost it at the station. The spot she'd put Keith in... She closed her eyes and wished for the floor to swallow her up. Keith might have hurt her with his distance and his relationship with Stacey, but he hadn't deserved to be outed in front of his colleagues and friends like that.

She swung her leg over the side of the bed and ran a hand through her sleep-mussed hair. She steeled her spine. Enough hiding. Time to face him and apologize.

With more confidence than she possessed, she padded down the stairs in her stocking feet and came to a halt on the bottom step. Keith's low timbre filtered through the house.

"You know, Carter, we have a lot of time to make up for. I know your mommy had her reasons, but I sure wish she would have told me."

Amy peeked around the corner.

Keith sat with his son snuggled in his arm, the sling awkwardly laid over Carter's belly.

"Ah, buddy, what am I going to do? I messed things up royally with your aunt Amy—or do I call her your momma? Are you as confused as I am?" He bent and kissed the baby on the top of his head.

A lump grew in Amy's throat. She had intruded on a private moment, but she couldn't leave.

"Carter, how do I make things right?"

The little boy blew raspberries, and tiny bubbles formed on his lips.

Keith chuckled. "I don't think being cute will work for me the way it works for you." He leaned his head back, closed his eyes and rocked his son.

The two made a beautiful picture of father and son. But where did she fit into the image? She'd played the part of a mother figure for Carter for what amounted to his entire life. Now she was second place to the child's dad.

Straightening her shoulders, she slipped into the room and sat near him on the couch.

Carter saw her and started babbling. Tears stung her eyes. The near-death experience had her aching to hold him. She wasn't used to sharing.

The easy chair stopped moving.

She glanced up. Her gaze connected with Keith's.

"I'm sure he's missed you. Go ahead, take him."

She willed her arms to stay at her sides. "You need time to bond. Really, it's okay."

"Ams. He needs you."

His words were all the invitation she needed. She scooped up Carter, buried her face in his sweet baby neck and inhaled his fresh powder scent. Her world settled, and her muscles relaxed.

"Feel better?" Keith eased back onto the recliner.

"Yes. Thank you." She sat Carter on her lap and gave him a rattle that promptly went into his mouth. "I owe you an apology."

Keith's brow raised.

"Don't look so surprised. I admit when I'm wrong. I shouldn't have taken my frustrations out on you. And I definitely shouldn't have done it in front of your coworkers."

His lips pulled into a taut line. "They're not just my coworkers, but my friends. It wasn't the way I wanted them to find out about Carter."

"I know. I truly am sorry. I was exhausted and overwhelmed. My life is completely out of focus. But that's still no excuse."

His chest rose and fell. The clock ticked in the background, and Carter slurped on his toy. She waited on Keith to respond, but her childhood friend remained silent.

The knowledge that they had no future together hurt, especially after he'd broken her heart by choosing her sister. But another door had closed on any chance she had of fulfilling her dream that had him front and center. And this time, she was the one who'd slammed it shut.

Amy tucked her face behind Carter and peered over his head. "Please, say something."

"I suppose, after all I've done, I can't hold it against you." He rubbed his eyes with his thumb and forefinger. "Apology accepted."

"Thank you." She breathed a sigh of relief. Maybe they'd find their way back to a solid friendship before this was over.

"I think we need to talk about Carter and Stacey." His grim tone caused her to cringe.

And like that, her sense of hope vanished. "Please. Not now. I can't take any more today." One more thing, and her nerves might snap.

Keith's phone beeped. He glanced at the text message, then back to her, and nodded. "All right. That conversation can wait." He held up the phone. "That was Jason. Letting me know all is clear outside."

"That's good." She hated friction between her and Keith. If only they could go back to before all the mistakes in their lives. Back to a childhood full of exploring and fun.

Keith shifted forward in his seat. "Amy, we need to retrieve the SD card. We have to put an end to this."

She wanted to be free from the insanity but giving up the final piece of evidence terrified her. Trusting Keith had always been as easy as taking a breath, but he'd given her the cold shoulder for a year, and even though she now knew why, she hesitated to agree. But if she wanted to find her attacker and Stacey's killer, she had to trust him. "Fine. I have to make a call. We can go in a couple of days once you're feeling better."

"Tomorrow, Ams. We go tomorrow." He stood and brushed a hand over Carter's hair. "I'm going to check on Jason."

She watched him stroll from the room. Her easygoing friend had disappeared, and a broken man determined to protect her had taken his place. Amy prayed Keith didn't get himself killed because of her. She wouldn't survive if she was responsible for someone else's death.

SIX

By the time Keith convinced Amy he felt good enough to drive, the traffic to Jackson had thinned enough to help spot a tail. Amy's tenacity had emerged, and he had to chuckle. He'd always appreciated that about her. The woman had strong-willed written all over her, but her sweet, shy demeanor softened her stubbornness.

Amy's familiar vanilla scent wafted on the air blowing from the air conditioner. A pang tugged at his heart. How had they grown so far apart in such a short time? As if he had to ask. The blame landed squarely on his shoulders.

Open fields and groves of trees zipped by, giving the feeling that danger didn't lurk, ready to pounce when they least expected it. "Where are we heading?" He flashed a glance at Amy. "Besides Jackson."

Her eyes darted from mirror to mirror and then to Carter in the back seat. "You're right, we should have left him with your dad."

That was what Keith had wanted, but he'd only been a father for three days. What did he know? On the other hand, they had to pull patrol from the house during the day. The department was too small to have him with Amy and someone with Carter.

"He'll be fine. We watch our backs, get the SD card and go straight home."

She bit her nail and nodded. "430 East King Street."

He blinked at the abrupt shift back to the address. Sometimes he couldn't keep up with Amy's change in thoughts.

"More specifically?" Keith drummed his fingers on the steering wheel. His left arm remained in his lap. Even with the sling, he was thankful that doc had taped his shoulder to relieve the pressure. Another day or two, and it shouldn't hurt as badly. His SIG Sauer hugged his right hip, giving him a sense of control.

"Stacey's attorney's office. It won't take long." Amy bit her bottom lip. "Do you want me to run in, and you stay with Carter?"

"No. We go together. I don't want you alone."

"And I don't want Carter in danger."

Too late for that. He bit back his response and drove in silence while he listened to Amy chatter with his son. A son he knew nothing about. He blinked at the sudden thought. He'd been so floored about his name on Carter's birth certificate, he hadn't looked at the date. "When's his birthday?"

Amy shifted against the door to face him. "January first."

He grinned. "A New Year's baby?"

"Yes. Stacey wasn't happy to be in the hospital on New Year's Eve."

"Sounds like her. She loved the holidays." Stacey had forced him and Amy to celebrate every holiday on the calendar during their teen years. He could only imagine her response at being in the hospital and not out ringing in the New Year.

Amy bit her bottom lip and lowered her gaze. "I'm sorry. I forgot you don't know these things."

He shrugged. Yes, he had a lot of time to make up for, but he couldn't change the past. He hadn't intentionally shirked his responsibility, but he felt like a loser dad all the same. He took a deep breath. "I assume you were there. How was—did she have a difficult time having Carter?"

"Actually, it was relatively easy."

He raised a brow. She had to be kidding. He had no doubt Stacey had had another opinion on the subject.

Amy laughed. "No. Really. She even said so. Her labor was short, and she took advantage of the pain meds."

"That's good. I'm glad. I feel horrible I wasn't

there for her." And he would have supported her every step of the way. Even if the whole time he longed for it to be with Amy and not Stacey.

"I guess she kept us both in the dark on that one. I still don't understand why she didn't tell me." The hurt returned to Amy's tone.

There were so many questions he wanted to ask, but he'd drop the topic for now. Stacey had hurt both of them, and it would take time to find solid footing again. Besides, he had to stay focused and alert. After the incident with his brakes, he couldn't allow himself the luxury of relaxing. He scanned the road one more time before taking the exit onto Second Street. The blue sedan two cars back bothered him. He merged onto the off-ramp. The car continued to stay behind them. His grip on the wheel tightened.

"Keith?"

"I think we have a tail. I'm going to take the long route and try to lose him." He glanced in the rearview mirror. The car seat caught his attention. Why hadn't he tried harder to convince Amy to leave Carter in Valley Springs? He could have asked one of the ladies from church to babysit.

Keith zigzagged through town and made it through a stoplight at the perfect time. The sedan had to stop, and Keith took advantage of the opportunity.

Ten minutes later, he pulled into a parking spot

in front of Smith and Schultz Attorneys at Law. "Let's hurry. I want to get out of town before whoever's in that blue car finds us again."

Amy unbuckled Carter, and they rushed inside.

After retrieving the package, Keith's hand hovered over his holstered SIG Sauer as they exited the building. He scanned the area and hustled Amy to the truck. Standing at the rear passenger door, he blocked Amy and his son with his body. His protective streak ratcheted up a notch. Anyone wanting to get to them would have to go through him first.

With Amy and Carter secure inside, he slipped around the front of the vehicle and got in.

The tension in his muscles ignited a burning ache in his injured shoulder. He rolled his neck from side to side as he got back on the road. "Is it in there?"

Amy opened the envelope and whimpered.

"Ams?" He glanced at her and returned his attention to the road.

"It's here. I guess I thought that whoever's after me might have gotten their hands on it." She folded the flap over on the small manila envelope and tucked it into the diaper bag.

The thought had crossed his mind, too.

Tall buildings zipped by as Keith maneuvered through town. He made his way onto the highway. The familiar landscape on either side of the road gave him hope of returning to Valley Springs without incident.

A blue sedan flashed in his mirror, and all his optimism disappeared. Their tail had returned. Keith punched speed dial on the cell phone cradled on the dash. He prayed his partner picked up.

"Cooper."

"Jason, I need backup on highway twelve. Mile marker two fifty-one, heading toward Valley Springs."

"Got it. Be there in five."

Keith ended the call. "Hang on. Jason will be here soon."

"He's ten miles out. How's he getting here in five minutes?" Amy's fingers curled around the door handle. "He'll never make it that fast."

Even with the tension building in the vehicle, a belly laugh burst from Keith. "My partner is known for his lead foot. Trust me, he'll be here." Jason had a reputation for driving like Mario Andretti, and right now, Keith was glad. With a quick glance to confirm the car's location, he sobered and slipped the sling from his left arm. If he had to confront the person following them, he wanted both arms available.

Blue lights flashed in the distance. "There's Jason. Hold on." He jerked the wheel to the right, pulled to the side of the road, and smashed on his brakes. "Stay here." He pulled his weapon and jumped from the vehicle.

"Keith!" Amy's voice muted as he slammed the door shut and rushed to the front of the truck to take cover.

Whoever the guy was, he'd never get close to Amy and Carter—Keith promised that.

"Carter, your stupid father is going to get himself killed." Amy climbed over the seat and slipped in next to her child. She froze. What was Carter to her now? When Stacey died, Amy thought she'd become Carter's mom and his only parent for the rest of his life. Where did she stand now? Technically, he wasn't even hers since Stacey had added Keith's name to the birth certificate. She kissed his cheek. How could she ever let him go?

The whine of sirens got closer. She looked over the edge of the seat and spotted not one but two sheriff's vehicles.

The officers blocked the road and took position behind their truck and SUV.

Her gaze shifted to the sedan that had followed them from Jackson. It flipped a U-ey, spun out and sped back the way it came. She released a pent-up breath and unbuckled Carter.

Her memory of Keith, Stacey and her came back like a splash of cold water. They'd grown up together and had always had each other's backs until that celebration a year ago. The one she'd left early and that had changed her life forever. The whole situation stunk. But at least they had survived the latest attempt on her life.

The guys had moved their vehicles to the side of the road and stood there deep in conversation. It shocked her to see that Sheriff Monroe had joined Jason in response to Keith's call.

She slid out of the truck and headed toward the small group of men.

"Gentlemen." She stepped next to Keith.

"Ms. Baker." Dennis nodded.

"Again, please make it Amy. I can't thank you enough for coming." She turned to Jason. "And thanks for patrolling last night and getting here so quickly."

Keith smirked. "Yeah, I'm a bit curious who had the heavier foot today."

Jason's eyes flew to Dennis, and he snorted. "I think boss man had me this time."

Amy bounced Carter and patted him on the back while she listened to the men debrief what had happened.

Keith's gaze drifted to his son. The look of terror had eased, but the desire to protect was evident. He craved to hold his son whether he realized it or not.

The idea of letting go of Carter made her heart

ache, but his father needed him. Amy nudged Keith and handed him the little boy. "Can you take him? He's getting heavy. Guess I'm still worn-out from yesterday."

"Sure." Keith sent her a confused look and cuddled his son against his chest.

The corner of Sheriff Monroe's mouth hitched. He hadn't missed her motives.

Keith rubbed tiny circles on Carter's back as the guys continued their conversation.

The slight breeze in the summer air ruffled the fine strands of hair on the baby's head. Amy longed for her camera. Her fingers itched to snap the image of father and son.

The scent of warm asphalt jolted her back to reality. Someone had followed them with less-than-honorable intentions, and there she stood on the side of the highway listening to three law enforcement officers discuss the tail and what to do next.

"Ready?" Keith lifted his son higher on his good shoulder. "I think we should get little man out of the heat."

Amy nodded and helped Keith buckle Carter into the car seat.

Instead of heading to the station for the formal statement, Jason followed them to Keith's house, and Dennis promised to join them after he dropped by the station.

Once at the house, Amy sank into the recliner with Carter cradled in her arms, slurping on a bottle. His eyes fluttered closed, and the sucking slowed.

Jealous of Carter's ability to relax and trust, Amy wondered if she'd ever feel completely at peace again. The day had taken a toll on her nerves. She needed all this to end—soon.

Statements given, Keith stepped out onto his back porch and collapsed onto a wooden rocker. Amy had put Carter down for a nap, and he'd insisted she join the infant while he slept.

"There you are."

Keith rolled his head to the left. Jason stood there, hands in his front pockets. "You found me. What's up?" He adjusted the sling to relieve the pull on his muscles.

"Thought you might want to chat."

Keith rolled his eyes. "Your wife's rubbing off on you."

"Dude." Jason glared at him.

"Sorry. It's been a long day."

"More than one." His partner lowered himself into the adjacent rocker.

"Truth." No denying it. The past few days seemed like a month—or two. "Guess I owe you an explanation."

"No. But I'll listen if you want to tell me."

Leave it to his friend to give him an out. He'd love to take it, but his friend deserved the whole story.

The screen door creaked and clicked closed.

"Had a feeling this is where I'd find you." Dennis moved to the steps and took a seat. The man had transformed from Keith and Jason's boss to a concerned friend.

Over the past few years, the group had learned to maneuver the shift between treating Dennis like the sheriff he was and a friend they hung out with. Not always easy, but Keith respected the man both as his superior and on a personal level.

Keith's gaze darted from one man to the other. "What is this? An intervention?"

Dennis chuckled. "Not unless you need one."

"So, gonna tell us, or are we going to talk about last night's Cleveland Guardians baseball game?" Jason crossed his ankle over his knee and picked at a thread on the hem of his tactical pants.

Keith sighed. No reason not to tell his friends other than his pride. "It all started a little over a year ago. Ams, Stacey and I were best friends growing up, so when Stacey received a military promotion, the three of us went out to celebrate." His heart grew heavy at the memories dancing in his mind. He'd lost so much over the past year. And a good portion of it was his own fault. "Amy left the celebration early, and the owner of the place brought out a bottle of champagne. Let's just say Stacey and I didn't have a faith to lean on and made a few poor decisions. I couldn't face Amy, so I never returned our normal phone calls or text messages."

He ran a hand through his hair and continued. "Fast-forward to three months ago, Stacey is murdered, and Amy disappeared. I had no idea Stacey had been pregnant. From what I can tell, she stayed quiet to save me from the shame of our bad judgment. I wish she'd told me. Anyway, Stacey hadn't told Amy either, so when Stace's estate attorney gave Amy an envelope, it contained the truth in black and white." Keith stared off into the late-afternoon sky and cradled his sore arm. "And boom, I'm a dad."

Birds chirped, and leaves rustled in the light breeze. The guys sat in silence. A quiet Keith appreciated. No quick admonishments, no knee-jerk advice.

Dennis spoke first. "That's rough."

"Yeah, tell me about it." Keith inhaled the fresh air, hoping it would clear the muddled mess in his brain.

"We all make mistakes. Don't beat yourself up. Don't let it negatively dictate your choices." Dennis's voice cracked. He cleared his throat.

"Love your son. Give him a great life. Be the best father you can possibly be."

Jason's eyes narrowed. His gaze shifted from Keith to Dennis. "Sounds like you're speaking from experience."

Dennis scratched his jaw and ignored Jason's comment. "What about Amy?"

"What about her?"

"Oh please," Jason piped in. "You get that dopey look every time she's around." He made a sappy puppy dog face.

Dennis chuckled. "You do that a little too well there, my friend."

"He does, doesn't he." Keith bit back a smile and listened to his friends banter.

God had given him great friends and coworkers. Guys he trusted with his life. But could Keith trust them with Carter's and Amy's? What choice did he have? Besides, God was in control, not him, or Jason, or Dennis.

They had taken an initial look at the photos, which confirmed her story and identified Debbie Ackers as the woman Amy had seen shot and fall over the cliff. But the images hadn't revealed the killer's identity, so tomorrow, he'd take Amy back to where the whole mess started and see if the surroundings jogged any details in her memory.

The idea turned his gut. He had no desire to

torture her with reliving the horrific event, but they needed a break in the case.

He scanned the backyard, wondering if Amy's attacker lurked within the trees that edged his property. Watching and waiting. Ready to eliminate the only witness.

SEVEN

Amy pulled up the pictures from the SD card the next morning, and after coming up empty—again—she sighed and gave in to the inevitable. Keith wanted to take her to the cliff so she could walk him through the events. She wasn't a fan of the idea, especially considering they'd ended up in the river the last time they attempted the drive, but he insisted he needed a visual of the crime scene.

A couple hours later, Amy sat in the passenger seat of the truck. Her muscles tightened at the pop of gravel beneath the truck tires. She stared out the window as Keith followed the winding path to the parking lot located at the trailhead. Sunlight filtered through the towering trees that lined the road. He pulled into a parking spot in the same lot where she had escaped with her life.

A glance around the area sparked Amy's memory. She hadn't returned to the site since she'd run from the killer three months ago. And she hadn't wanted to come back now. Her erratic emotions pinged like a pinball.

She slipped from Keith's truck and ambled to the trailhead. Her heartbeat pounded and sweat beaded on her forehead. How could a simple location cause panic to edge in? The panic attacks that had plagued her since Stacey's death had vanished since she'd had Keith by her side. But one look at the dirt path, and her body threatened to revolt.

"You doing okay?" Keith put his arm around her shoulder. He'd left the sling at home, said two days was long enough. However, Amy noticed he hadn't removed the tape stabilizing his muscles.

"I'm not sure I want to do this." She straightened her spine. "But I don't have a choice. You need to see it."

He slipped his hand into hers and squeezed. "I'm here, and I'm armed. Besides, I have Jason on lookout down the road. No one is going to come into the parking lot without him noticing."

Keith beside her and Jason backing him up gave Amy a small sense of peace. Maybe she could do this without falling apart. "Let's get this over with." She strode up the path, her breath whooshing in her ears.

"Tell me more about Carter." Keith matched her pace.

She gazed at him. "Trying to get my mind off this excursion by distracting me?"

"Is that a bad thing?" He smiled at her. "Besides, I'd like to hear about my son."

And there it was, the wedge between them. Keith deserved to know, and someday she'd have to let go of the hurt of being the wrong twin, coming in second once again. "He's an easy baby. Never has been a problem. He loves to eat, and as your dad pointed out, he's a noisy eater at that."

"I know he's only four months old, but does he have favorites?"

She nodded. "Stacey gave him a stuffed elephant that he loves."

"The one next to his crib?"

"Exactly. He has a special blanket, too. I found a matching one and interchange them, so if I lose one, the world won't come to an end."

Keith chuckled. "Good plan." He tugged her to a stop.

"What is it?" Panic clawed up her throat.

"We're here." He gestured toward the open landscape filled with flowers of every color.

Unbelievable. She'd hiked up the trail without realizing it. "Oh, you are good." Amy released his hand and spun in a slow circle. "Over there." She pointed to a wooded area with a clear view of the cliff.

They trudged to her original spot. "I knelt here

and set up my shot toward the rocks. The snow had an ice layer that glistened. I wanted to capture the pristine ground against the rugged rock forms." She held her hands out in an L shape and framed the shot.

"From the landscape images I saw earlier, you have some amazing photos."

"Yeah, well, a lot of good they're doing stuck on that memory card. I can't make a living without displaying them at the art gallery."

"What happened next?"

"See that clearing?" She pointed to the area where the wildflowers met the rocks.

"Yes."

"I aimed at the lake beyond the drop-off. That's when I saw a woman..." Her lower lip trembled at the memory.

"Debbie Ackers."

Amy nodded. "...Debbie held at gunpoint. The guy had his back to me, and a hoodie covered his head." She stood and meandered to the cliff's edge. The event ran in her mind like a film reel. "He held the gun to her head..." Amy held her fingers in the shape of a gun and held them to Keith's forehead. "And pulled the trigger. Debbie tumbled over the cliff." Amy rubbed her arms, trying to chase away the chill in the air that didn't exist.

Keith tugged her close and wrapped his arms around her waist. "It's okay. I've got you, Ams."

She rested her head on his shoulder and inhaled his scent. His musky cologne mixed with the odor of exertion. He smelled good. She almost laughed. Amy and her sister had spent hours making fun of romance stories that talked about how a sweaty guy smelled good. Now— she had to agree. It made her feel safe.

His gaze met hers. "I'm sorry you had to experience that." Keith's eyes searched hers. His gaze dropped to her lips, and he leaned in.

A kiss from him would be a dream come true. But she couldn't let it happen. He'd betrayed her, and she wouldn't allow herself to fall for him. She stepped back. "Keith. I can't."

Something whizzed past her face.

"Get down!" Keith threw her to the ground and landed on top of her.

What was that? Her lungs refused to fill with air. "Can't breathe." He shifted his weight, and she sucked in precious oxygen.

"We have to get out of here."

Amy's gaze darted around the area. Everywhere she looked made them an open target. They were pinned down. "Where?"

"Down the cliff. It's our only option." He yanked her to the edge and ducked behind a boulder seconds before another shot pinged in the dirt where she had just stood. "We used to rock climb at the gym all the time during high school."

"What about your arm? You can't climb, let alone free solo climb. You'll fall." She had to think—come up with another plan. It didn't matter the cliff face was only about three stories high. She feared he'd fall to his death, and she'd lose another person she cared for.

Another bullet pinged on the rock above her head.

"We don't have much choice. My shoulder's still taped, so I have some support." He gestured to a dip in the rock then pulled his weapon. "Get over the edge and start down-climbing. I'll cover you."

Against her better judgment, she cupped his cheek and met his gaze. "Please don't get hurt."

His hand spanned the back of her head. He pulled her close and kissed her forehead. "Not a chance. Go." He popped up and fired.

She sprinted the short distance, found footholds and started her descent. Five feet down, she glanced up to find Keith following the same path she'd taken. They had to hurry. The killer had to be close behind.

Handhold after toehold, she rhythmically made her way down the rock front.

Pausing for a moment, she looked up. "You doing okay?"

"I'm—" Keith slipped. He hung by a single-handed grip, pain etching his face.

"Keith!" He was going to die all because she'd called him for help.

Keith's heart threatened to beat from his chest as he dangled by his right hand. He fought to regain his grip and find footholds. His left hand found purchase, but his weight pulled at his damaged muscles. Scrambling for footholds, he prayed the loose rocks he'd sent tumbling down the side hadn't hurt Amy.

"Keith!"

He groaned at the pain pulsing in his shoulder. He gritted his teeth. "Keep going."

"Are you okay?"

"Go. Before he finds us." Keith blew air through pursed lips. *Lord, give me the strength to make it down this rock and keep Amy safe.*

Each foot took what felt like an hour to descend. When he reached the bottom, Amy grabbed his hand and pulled him into a small cove.

He fell to the ground and propped himself against the wet rock. Tucked under the overhang, he slid his SIG from his holster and placed it in his lap. The adrenaline had faded, and a fire had lit his shoulder. Rock climbing hadn't exactly been on his doctor's to-do list when the man told

Keith to take it easy. Nausea roiled in his stomach, and spots danced in his vision. He inhaled through his nose and continued to pray the pain away. Where was his partner?

Amy knelt beside him and brushed the sweat-matted hair from his forehead. "What can I do?"

This woman had known him his entire life. He couldn't hide his discomfort from her and had no reason to. "Keep an eye out. Give me a minute, then we'll call Jason and find out what happened and have him come get us." He closed his eyes, willing the ache to subside.

The rocky sand shifted next to him. Amy had moved away. He missed her closeness, her gentle touch. What would it be like to have her next to him every day, facing life together?

"Jason, we had to down-climb the rock face. You have to come get us. There's no way Keith can go back up." Amy's voice snapped him back to the situation at hand.

Of course she had taken control and called for help. It was her nature to take charge in a quiet way. Stacey bulldozed her way through life. Amy had a softer approach, but she'd find a need and get things done. He appreciated her gentler style.

The soreness started to subside. Keith opened his eyes. His gaze landed on Amy pacing within the cove, staying out of sight from above. The amazing woman in front of him made his heart flutter. If he hadn't blown things, maybe he would've had a chance with her. Something he'd wanted for years. But he had to face the fact that she deserved a better man than him.

"Yes, he's fine." She paused and ran her gaze over his shoulder, inspecting the damage. "He'll be sore, but it's still in place." Amy pivoted, took a step and crouched at the edge of the rock formation.

A scream pierced the air.

Keith scrambled to his feet and staggered to Amy. "What's wron—" A partially skeletonized body lay next to the boulders, half-buried beneath the rocky sand. He scooped up her phone and drew her away from the corpse.

"What's going on?" Jason's heavy breathing indicated he was running.

"I think we found Debbie Ackers." Keith ambled to where he'd sat moments ago with Amy in tow.

"I'm on my way."

"What about the shooter?"

"Gone. I chased him through the woods but lost him. He came up that old hunter's trail on the other side that no one uses anymore."

Why hadn't they thought of that? Pure and simple. Few people knew about it. And they'd blown it.

"Hang tight. I'll grab Melanie, and we'll head in from the lakeside."

"Thanks. See ya soon." Keith lowered himself to the ground before he fell down. Amy joined him, and he pulled her to his chest and smoothed his hand down her hair. "Shh. It's okay. I've got you." Her tears broke his heart. No one should witness what she'd seen.

Keith glanced upward at the rock face they'd descended to escape the person intent on killing Amy. They'd barely survived. How would he keep her safe if the murderer continued to come after her?

EIGHT

After arriving home, Amy had ordered Keith to shower while she gave Ian a break and fed Carter. The taut muscles in Keith's face had told her how much pain he was in. She insisted he clean up and relax before he collapsed from the taxing down-climb. When he joined her downstairs, she'd pointed him to the recliner and gave him an ice pack. Keith hadn't objected, another sign of how much he hurt. He'd kicked up the footrest and leaned back. Amy placed a sleepy Carter on his chest and left the two alone.

Thirty minutes later, Amy ran her fingers through her wet hair, thankful for a hot shower and comfortable clothes. Her arms and legs ached. She hadn't rock climbed in years. The physical exertion had worn her out, and stress added another layer.

Firm grip on the handrail, she descended the stairs like a hundred-year-old grandmother. Stepping into the living room, her gaze drifted to

Keith and Carter. The baby lay belly down on Keith's shoulder and chest, his thumb hanging loosely between his gums. Her childhood friend's cheek rested on Carter's head, and the ice pack she'd filled earlier had liquefied. Soft snores from both filled the otherwise silent room. The picture of the two eased her tension. She could watch them all day long.

"They make a pair, don't they?"

Her hand flew over her heart. "Ian, you scared me."

"Sorry about that. Would you like some tea?" He motioned toward the kitchen.

"Absolutely. My nerves haven't settled yet from our…adventure." That was one way to put it. Fight for their life described it better, but she had chosen not to drown in terror.

"I'm not surprised. Before my son fell asleep, he gave me a quick rundown of what happened." The older man busied himself, filling the teakettle and prepping mugs.

The scent of cinnamon and apple wafted in the air. Ian had baked apple crisp, and the dish sat cooling on the stove.

Amy glanced out the window, wondering if the person responsible for shooting at them waited out there for another opportunity.

"Don't worry, darlin'. Dennis is on protection duty. No one will get by the sheriff."

She pivoted to face Keith's father and hugged her waist. "I can't believe he's taking a shift. Shouldn't he assign someone else? I mean, he's the boss, right?"

Ian laughed. "Oh, Dennis is the boss all right, but with him being young and so close in age to his deputies, he runs the office a little different."

Grateful for the distraction, she pulled out a chair and sat down. A moan escaped her lips. Man, she was sore. "That has to be weird for everyone involved."

Ian gave her a sympathetic smile. He placed a cup on the table and took a seat across from her. "No, not really. They make it work. Everyone seems happy with the setup."

"That's good." She ran her finger around the rim of her mug. She was happy that her friend had found a job he loved and a group of supportive friends. The claws of loneliness gripped her. She missed her friends, her sister, her life.

Ian placed his hand on her forearm. "You've had a lot going on lately. Remember, I'm here if you need to talk."

A lump formed in her throat. She'd grown up with Ian as a second father, and he was all she had left. The fact he'd offered meant the world to her. She patted his hand. "Thank you. With my parents gone, and now Stacey…"

"I understand. When Keith's mother died, I

was lost there for a while, but Keith insisted I come live here with him. I have to admit, he was right. I can't imagine rattling around in that big house without my sweet Leah. I will always be grateful to my son for sparing me from the loneliness."

"When Stacey was killed, I didn't know what to do. Suddenly I was hiding from a madman with an infant who had no one but me." Tears pooled on her lashes. "Ian, I'm so sorry Stacey kept Carter from you and Keith. I don't know what my sister was thinking."

"I've known you girls most of your life. It baffles me, too. But I wonder if she was trying to protect Keith in her own way. His mother was dying. Keith regrets his actions, as I'm sure Stacey did. She was probably trying to make the best out of their poor choices." The older man lifted the mug to his lips and drained the brown liquid. "That girl liked to do things her own way, but I doubt she set out to hurt any of us."

"Maybe you're right." She prayed her twin's motives were that noble. "I still think it was selfish. She's put me in an awkward situation. I'm Carter's legal guardian, but now that she's had his birth certificate updated, Keith is legally his father. Within the law, I don't know where that puts us." Amy tightened her grip on her cup in hopes of stopping her hands from trembling. She took a sip of tea then inhaled a deep breath. Carter was hers, and Amy had no idea what she'd do if Keith took her baby from her.

Ian stood, patted her shoulder then ambled to the teakettle. "My son will do right by his child— and you. Carter needs a mother. Keith knows that."

The man could read her mind. And she prayed he was right.

He refilled his mug and returned to his seat. "But that's not all that's bothering you, is it?"

What did Amy say to that? Anger filled her insides at the thought that Stacey and Keith had a relationship, even if only for one night. How did she admit that to Ian? "No, it's not. But it's weird talking with you since you're Keith's father."

"Darlin', consider me your family, too."

"Thank you. You've always been special to me." She placed her hand on Ian's. "Ian, why did they do it? Why them?" Her real question died on her lips.

The older man's eyes searched hers. "Why not you? That's what you really want to know. Isn't it?"

Amy stared at Ian, her mouth gaped open. How could he possibly know that?

The corner of the older man's mouth curved upward. "I've seen the way you look at my son. And I've seen him look at you the same way."

She shook her head. Ian was wrong. "He's never—"

The father figure across from her chuckled. "Oh yes, he has."

"Well, it doesn't matter. Stacey and I are—were—identical twins. He chose her. Not me. That should tell you who he really wanted." Amy couldn't believe she was sitting at a table with Keith's father discussing the awkward topic.

"Oh, honey, I think he made a huge mistake, and he knows it."

"Who knows what?" Keith stood in the kitchen doorway, hair sleep mussed.

Heat rushed up Amy's neck. How much had Keith heard? She prayed he'd just walked in. Ian gave her a lopsided smile. If she could beg the floor to swallow her whole, she would.

"We—uh—" She deflected his question with one of her own. "Where's Carter?"

Keith quirked a brow, silently challenging her motives behind the question.

He could take that good-looking lazy grin and stuff it. Amy wasn't backing down. "Well?"

"He's still asleep, so I tossed a blanket on the floor and laid him down." Keith ambled to the freezer and grabbed another ice pack. His shoulder smarted, and Carter was heavier than he looked.

"How's the arm?"

"Sore. The climb did a number on it, but it'll heal." He plopped down beside his father and situated the cold bag on his shoulder. "Pops, you think you could keep an eye on champ tomorrow morning so Ams and I can go pay a visit to the mayor? I'd like to drop by the café and see what he has to say about his assistant."

"You want to see his response in a casual setting while his professional demeanor is down, don't you?" His dad leaned back and folded his arms across his chest.

"Yup. I'm interested in what his excuse is for Debbie's disappearance from town."

Ian grinned. "Sure. I'd love to spend time with my grandson. The boy needs to be spoiled."

Amy gave an exaggerated groan. "Just great. That's all I need."

All *she* needed? Carter was his son, and if Pops wanted to spoil him, so be it. They had both missed out on four months of Carter's life thanks to Stacey's silence. Then again, what did he know about raising a child? He'd had the role of father thrust on him for less than a week. No. He'd been a father for four months, he just hadn't known about it.

He scratched the stubble on his jaw. "I'm sure Pops won't go overboard with the spoiling. Will you?" he challenged his father.

"Only a little." Ian slapped the table. "Why don't I get out of here so you two can make a plan."

Keith's gaze followed his dad's path as the man

meandered into the living room, leaving him and Amy alone. His attention returned to the beautiful woman across from him. "So, what were you and my dad talking about?"

She rubbed at an invisible spot on the table. "Not much."

"Really? Seemed rather intense."

"Ian offered to listen if I ever wanted to talk. That's all."

Keith knew there was more to it, but when Amy clammed up, all the prodding in the world wouldn't get her to talk. He grabbed the ice pack off his shoulder and tossed it in the sink. The hard cubes clanged against the stainless steel. Cringing, he listened for Carter's cry. He released a breath when no sound came from the infant.

Hand covering her mouth, Amy's shoulders bounced with her quiet laughter. "You should have seen your face."

He rolled his eyes, but a curve pulled on the corner of his lips. "Now that you've had your fun let's take a better look at those pictures. I like to be prepared and have all the facts before I question a suspect."

"You think the mayor did it?" Amy's eyes widened.

"If Debbie is the woman you saw killed—" He held a hand up to stop her comment. "I believe you, and the photos are proof. But if Debbie's the victim, I want to know why the mayor hasn't reported her missing. His reaction will tell us a lot."

"I never thought of that." She chewed on the inside of her cheek. "What's the plan?"

"Brunch at the café. The mayor, his family and his best friend, Christopher Dayton, meet there every day around eleven." Catching Mayor Taylor in a public place would allow Keith the upper hand by taking the man out of his power position.

"And you want to show up and ask him questions?" The creases in Amy's forehead deepened.

"I was thinking more along the lines of taking you to an early lunch and happening to run into him."

"Then it's a date." Pink rushed to her cheeks. "I—I mean, it sounds good to me."

Keith's brain whirled. A date? Amy hadn't meant to say it, but oh, how he'd like it to be true. Maybe if he'd taken a chance a few years ago and asked her out, he wouldn't have made the huge blunder with Stacey. But that was in the past, and right now, his chances of having a future with Amy were as slim as a piece of dental floss.

Time to change the subject before he said something to push her further away. "What do you say we print the photos from that SD card? I'd like to take a closer look."

"Sure, I'll go grab it." Amy didn't look sure.

The bags under her eyes and the droop of her shoulders told the story of the difficult days she'd lived through. She returned a few minutes later with her computer and memory card in hand.

"Thank you." Keith rose and took the offered laptop. He placed it on the table then pulled out her chair for her. "Have a seat. I'll let you set it up and print them. Then we can examine the evidence together."

Amy settled into her seat. She opened her laptop, signed in then snapped the SD card into the reader slot.

He linked her computer to the printer and hit Send.

While the images printed, he wandered to the kitchen window and glanced out. Jason had relieved Dennis at some point, making Keith wonder what had pulled his boss away. But the sight of his partner making his rounds eased the worry stirring inside Keith. With the guys from the station taking turns monitoring the house, he focused on Amy's safety. He'd remember to thank them later. Besides, his ability to protect her had decreased with his throbbing shoulder. He required help, now more than ever before. His friends had seen the need and stepped up in a big way. The vulnerability killed him, but life had thrown him multiple challenges, and he refused to put Amy in danger due to his stupid pride. But still… The hum of the refrigerator broke through his thoughts.

He pivoted and strode to Amy's side, pushing his inadequacies to the back of his mind. He had bigger problems than showing off. If Amy was right and Debbie Ackers had died that day, then Keith's investigation had just landed in a pool of political hot lava. The chances of the mayor or someone in his circle being involved increased drastically.

A warm breeze drifted through the open windows and door. The heat from the past week had dissipated, turning the warm summer day cool enough to allow the fresh air to drift in through the screens and fill the house. A wisp of Amy's hair escaped the ponytail and fluttered against her cheek. She slowly flipped through the photos and paused at the picture of Debbie Ackers's last moment. "It really was her."

Keith leaned over Amy's shoulder. Much too close for her sanity. "It was. And between the pictures and your statement, we have proof."

His warm breath tickled her neck, sending tingles up her spine. "I…um…" His proximity caused her brain waves to go haywire. She blinked and attempted to refocus. She had to get it together. She wasn't a lovesick teenager anymore. She was a grown woman who had control of her emotions. Right? Besides, he'd made his choice, and it hadn't been her. She refused to be anyone's second choice. "At least I know I was right and that my mind hadn't played tricks on me. It's just weird to see it in printed color."

"Lay the photos out on the table. I didn't see anything yesterday, but let's take a closer look and see if we can identify our killer."

"Good idea." Amy spread the images on the table as Keith slipped onto the seat next to her. His musky cologne and fresh soap smell wreaked havoc with her mind. She shook off the direction her thoughts had taken. "Here's a couple that might work."

They studied the two pictures, looking for any hint as to who the murderer might be.

"I've met Debbie on several occasions. I'd say she's about five foot six or seven." He pointed to a picture. "Our guy is a little taller. Maybe five-ten or eleven. If he's six foot, I'd be surprised."

"How tall is the mayor?" The information wasn't sufficient to find the person responsible but was significant enough to narrow down the list.

"About that." Keith shifted. His eyes met hers. "All the more reason we need to speak with him. I know you've already given the sheriff a copy, but can you select a few of the pictures and email them to me?"

Amy slid her laptop closer and wiggled the

mouse. "Let me filter through some of these images." She created a photo gallery of the top pictures that contained Debbie and her assailant. "These are the best I have."

Keith leaned forward and studied the laptop screen. "That'll work. Send them to me and copy the sheriff on these specific images if you would, please."

"Sure." She typed in the email addresses he dictated to her and attached the photos to the message.

The screen door creaked open and slammed shut. Jason waltzed in and went straight to the cabinet. "I had to relieve the boss man for a bit. He had something come up, but Kyle's here now." He pulled out a glass and filled it with iced tea from the refrigerator, then joined them at the table and plopped onto one of the chairs. Keith's partner lifted the drink and drained half of the liquid. With an exaggerated sigh, he set his glass down with a clunk. Jason folded his hands over his stomach. His gaze darted from her to Keith. "You guys find anything good?"

Keith arched a brow. "Make yourself comfortable, why don't ya?"

"I did, thanks." Jason smirked. "By the way, Kyle said they dusted for prints at Detective Jefferies's house but don't expect to find anything.

Same with the hotel room. Nothing to go on. But he's still looking for leads in the investigation."

"Good to know. Hope something turns up soon."

Jason jutted his chin at the pictures. "So. Whatcha got?"

Keith shook his head at Jason's antics then filled him in with the information they'd discovered. "The pictures confirmed it was Debbie on the cliff. As soon as Melanie ID's the body, we can make it official."

"She's working on it. Otherwise, she'd be here with me right now." Jason took another sip of his drink.

"And we appreciate your sacrifice." Keith deadpanned the statement.

Amy wanted to laugh at the partners' interaction. It warmed her, knowing Keith had found such wonderful friends and coworkers. A pang struck her heart. It had once been her and Stacey who shared the teasing words and laughs with each other. Now, Stace was gone, and Amy and Keith's relationship had taken a direct hit. She pushed the jealousy from her thoughts. "Come see what you think."

Jason stood and moved behind her. With one hand on Keith's chair and the other on hers, Jason leaned between them and picked up a photo.

"Yup, that's Debbie all right." Jason waited as Amy handed him a picture of the attacker.

When he didn't respond, Amy peered up at him. "You know who it is?"

"No. But something does seem familiar. I just can't put my finger on it."

Keith switched to the computer, took the mouse and zoomed in on the hooded figure. "Anything strike you?"

"He's about the same height as the mayor, but…"

"But what?" Amy prompted.

"Something's off. Maybe it's the bulky clothes throwing me. I'm just not sure." Jason studied the photo a little longer then exhaled. He straightened, grabbed his glass and downed his tea. The ice cubes clunked in the empty glass. "I'll keep thinking on it. Sorry I couldn't be of more help."

Keith moved to the freezer, pulled out another ice pack and then leaned his hip against the counter. The tension in his jaw concerned Amy. The man had to be hurting. Yet he'd sat with her and discussed the case.

A wave of relief filled Keith's face when he held the ice pack to his shoulder. "That's okay. We plan to confront Mayor Taylor tomorrow at the café. See his reaction when we ask where Debbie is."

"Let me know what you find out." Jason

turned to Amy. "Make sure you call if you need anything "

Amy nodded. "Thanks. I doubt I'll need to since Keith is all but glued to my side, but I'm grateful for all you're doing for Carter and me."

"No problem. Besides, the little dude is as close to a nephew as I'm going to get. So gotta keep him safe." Jason smiled. "I'll catch you two later. I'm going to grab a few minutes of playtime with Carter and Ian. Kyle's here, for now, then Doug will replace him in a few hours or so for the night shift. Dennis will be back here around 3:00 a.m. until the sun comes up. We've got you covered."

Keith gave his partner a bro hug. "Thanks, man."

"That's what partners are for. You two get some rest. Y'all look like you need it." Jason strode out of the kitchen.

A minute later, baby giggles drifted in from the living room.

Keith's gaze never left the doorway. A smile tugged at his lips.

Her twin had really messed things up when she hadn't trusted her or Keith with the name of Carter's father. As much as it pained Amy to consider the consequences, she was glad they had discovered the truth.

Because if Amy's attacker succeeded in killing her, at least Carter would have his father.

NINE

Keith rolled his head to the side and glanced at the alarm clock. 9:00 a.m. He blinked and double-checked the time. He jolted up, instantly regretting the quick movement. His muscles had tightened overnight, and the ache in his shoulder reminded him of the agonizing ill-advised down-climb yesterday. Not that he had a choice. It was either that or be killed. But today the escape down the cliff had his body wondering if he'd aged forty years in the past twelve hours.

Amazed that Carter's cries hadn't woken him, he swung his legs over the edge of the bed and hung his head waiting for the discomfort to pass. Good thing he didn't need to impress Amy. She knew him and all his faults, including his biggest lapse in judgment with Stacey. But his inability to keep her safe so far hurt his pride the most. She'd rescued him and treated him on two occasions. Amy two, Keith zero. Some superhero lawman he was.

When the pain subsided, he grabbed the pain reliever on his nightstand and downed two tablets. He prayed by the time he showered and made it downstairs, he'd feel almost normal.

Twenty minutes and a shower and shave later, Keith hobbled downstairs, compliments of yesterday's climb. The scent of frying bacon and fresh biscuits filled the air. His mouth watered, and his stomach grumbled.

His gaze roamed the living room for Carter but came up empty. Giggles erupted from the kitchen. When he entered, he found Carter strapped in a high chair, happily sucking on a teething ring.

"There's my little man." Keith shuffled over and kissed the baby on the top of the head. His heart swelled at the big toothless grin he received in response.

The clank of plates to his right had him shifting his attention to the most beautiful woman in the world. He almost sighed in appreciation at the sight of her.

"You ready for breakfast, sleepyhead?" Amy's teasing tone made him smile.

Keith imagined waking up to her playfulness every morning. The idea warmed his insides but soon fizzled out. Amy had made it clear that her forgiveness didn't extend to his faux pas with her twin. Something he prayed she'd look past in the near future, but he wouldn't hold his breath.

"Sorry. I don't know what happened. I normally don't sleep that late. I should have been up to help you with Carter."

Spatula in hand, Amy popped her wrist on her hips. "You're injured and need time to heal. I'm used to taking care of Carter." The unspoken word *alone* hung in the air. "We're fine, and you'll get your fair share of parenthood soon enough."

"I'm sure I will." Keith ran a hand through his wet hair. "How did you escape unscathed from our adventure? I feel like I ran a Spartan Race."

She laughed and flipped the sizzling bacon in the pan. "Are you kidding? I can barely move my arms and legs."

At least he wasn't the only one. "Please, tell me how I can help." He inhaled the meaty aroma. He'd wash dishes for a month if she'd be generous with his helping.

"Right now, you can sit and drink a cup of coffee before your grumpy alter ego shows up."

"Yes, ma'am." So she hadn't forgotten his quirks. A thought that made him happier than he intended to admit.

"What time are we leaving for the café?" She filled a plate and placed it in front of him.

He sipped the dark brew, allowing the caffeine a chance to take hold. "I thought we'd arrive around 11:30 a.m. Give the mayor ample time to get comfortable with his family and best friend." Keith bit off a chunk of bacon, then pulled apart the steaming flaky biscuit Amy had placed on his plate and slathered it with butter. The biscuit melted in his mouth. "Wow, everything is so good."

"Thank you. I like to cook, but I don't get much of a chance since it's only Carter and me." Washcloth in hand, Amy wiped Carter's face. "By the way, I confirmed with Ian that he's available to watch Carter while we're gone."

He swallowed then wiped his mouth with his napkin. "I have a feeling Dad will take any opportunity to love on his grandson."

Amy's movements halted.

When would he learn not to push Carter's parentage? Each time Keith brought up the fact that Carter was his, Amy bristled. No doubt experiencing the hurt of his actions all over again.

She quickly cleaned the little guy, slid him from his high chair and held him close. "I'm sure he will. I've prepped lunch for the two of them." Tears glistened in Amy's eyes. She shoved Carter at Keith. "Here, take over your fatherly duty while I go get ready."

He dropped his fork and fumbled to hold his son.

Handoff made, Amy pivoted and hurried from the room.

"Well, little man. I think I stepped in horse manure with your aunt...your momma... I'm still not sure what to call her." The statement gave Keith pause. Now that Stacey had officially identified him as the baby's father, where did that leave Amy?

He didn't have time to ponder the legal implications. Because if they didn't discover and stop whoever intended to kill Amy, the issue was a moot point.

The short time away from Keith to dress and gather her thoughts had improved Amy's mood. Dealing with Carter's newfound parentage resembled walking across a frozen lake. One step, solid and comfortable. The next, a crackle and her foot plunging through the thin ice. She prayed she'd come to grips with the information and learn how to respond without hurtful words.

God, this one is on You. I don't know how to do that.

She sat in Keith's rental truck and watched the trees and flowers zip by.

Silence filled the cab as they made their way to the diner.

Slipping from the truck, Keith escorted her down the sidewalk and pushed open the door to the café. He gestured for her to go on in. Several patrons shifted their attention to the entrance and smiled. Keith raised a hand, acknowledging them, then placed his hand on her lower back, leading her toward the rear of the restaurant.

She stiffened at his touch. Her anger simmered beneath the surface. All these years, she'd wanted him to take her out on a date, treat her like a woman. Instead, he'd chosen her sister. The pain ran deep. But right now, they had a job to do. She swallowed her pride and shook off the betrayal. She had to focus on the reason they'd come to the diner. To face Mayor Taylor.

Amy leaned in and whispered, "You think he'll talk to us?"

"I don't intend to give him a choice." Keith pointed to a large table on the left. "Over there. Looks like everyone's here except his son, Trevor. Come on."

Amy clasped her shaking hands in front of her. Was she about to meet a murderer? She glanced back at the door. Her mind and body warred with each other, but Amy hadn't come this far to quit now. Stacey's killer deserved to be caught. Amy soaked in the strength from Keith's touch and held her head high.

Each step closer to Mayor Taylor's table felt like stepping off a cliff and plunging to her death.

"Try to relax. He won't hurt you with all these people around." Keith's breath tickled her ear.

Yeah, right. What about afterward with no

one as a witness? "I'm good." Not exactly, but she didn't have a choice. "Let's find out what he knows."

Keith flashed her a grin, and for a moment, her world settled.

Standing next to the mayor's table, Keith stuck out his hand. "Good morning, Mayor."

"Ah, Detective Young. Nice to see you." The mayor stood and shook Keith's hand. The man's eyes drifted to her. "And who is this lovely lady?"

She studied his eyes. No hint of worry or deception in them. "Amy. Amy Baker."

"It's nice to see Detective Young in such fine company."

"Thank you, sir." Funny. The man didn't repulse her like she'd expected. Maybe he poured on the syrupy sweetness too thick, but other than that, he seemed genuinely nice.

"Please, call me Nolan."

"All right, Nolan."

Mayor Taylor lowered himself onto his chair then shifted his attention to Keith. "And to what do I owe the honor of your visit?"

"I'm working on a case, and your assistant's name came up."

The man furrowed his brow. "Debbie?"

"Yes, sir. Do you know where she is?"

"Debbie? What about her?" A tall, younger version of the mayor patted him on the shoulder, then made his way to Sheila, the mayor's wife, and kissed her on the cheek. He then shook hands with Christopher Dayton, the mayor's best friend, and sat next to Sheila.

"This is my son, Trevor," the mayor said. "Trevor, I think you know Detective Young, and this is Ms. Baker."

Trevor nodded. "Nice to meet you." He unrolled his silverware and placed the napkin in his lap. "Now, what's this about Debbie?"

"I was just asking if your father knows where she is." Keith's gaze went from Trevor back to the mayor.

Mayor Taylor took a sip of his coffee and placed the cup on the table. "Why, yes I do. She's visiting her great-grandmother in Phoenix."

"How long has she been gone?"

"Around four months. Her nana, as she called her, broke her hip. Since the girl's mother and grandmother passed on, she requested time off to go and help." Mayor Taylor shrugged. "I granted it."

"That's awfully nice of you," Amy said. She noticed the way Nolan's voice softened when he spoke of Debbie. Not like a man hiding murder.

"Debbie's a sweet girl. A hard worker." He shrugged.

Keith remained all business. "So, she requested the time and left?"

Nolan's head tilted to the side. "No. Not exactly. As I recall, one day, we discussed her nana, and a few days later, she texted me that she needed to help the older woman. Said she'd keep me in the loop."

Keith crossed his arms. "And has she texted you since?"

"Yes. Once every couple of weeks. Gives me an update and thanks me for being so understanding." The mayor's gaze narrowed. "Detective, what are you fishing at?"

"Skeletal remains were found yesterday, and we have reason to believe it's her."

Nolan Taylor's voice rose. "Not possible. I texted with her yesterday."

Amy took a chance and placed her hand on Nolan's forearm. Confusion danced in his eyes. "Could we look at the message she sent you?" Amy hadn't waited on Keith. She had to see for herself.

"I can assure you the person isn't Debbie." Muscles twitched in the man's jaw.

"Mayor." Keith's tone softened. "I'm not saying you're lying. But it will help ease our worry if you showed us that text message."

"I don't know what you think you'll find, but I don't see any harm in showing you." Mayor Taylor extracted his cell phone from his pocket and tapped the screen a few times. "Since I use my phone for work, you can't have access to all my communications. But here's her last text and my response." He held the device out.

"Dad, I don't think that's a good idea." Trevor's voice held an edge to it.

The mayor waved him off. "Nonsense."

Trevor scowled at his father but kept his mouth shut.

Amy scanned the others at the table. Sheila, the mayor's wife, sat preoccupied with her cell phone, and the mayor's friend glanced around the table, then picked at his food.

Odd reactions for hearing that someone they knew could be dead.

His hand on the bottom of the phone to steady it, Keith's focus lasered in on the words.

Amy joined him, reading the text. Sure enough, Debbie's note said her nana had caught pneumonia, and it would be a while longer. She'd claimed she might have to stay indefinitely. Nolan's message clearly stated that her job would be there when she returned.

"Thank you." Keith nodded, and the mayor retracted his phone. "Had Debbie ever told you she wasn't coming back?"

"On several occasions she expressed concern as to how she'd take care of her nana long-term. But I told her not to worry, to take all the time she needed to work things out. That she'd have a place when she returned."

How thoughtful of him. But who did that? Especially someone in a political role who needed his staff present every day. Amy met Keith's gaze. If the mayor was telling the truth, someone had done a great job not raising any flags concerning Debbie's death.

The mayor's wife, Sheila, stood and kissed her husband on the cheek. "I'm sorry to eat and run, but I have an appointment." The elegant woman turned to Amy and Keith. "Nice to see you both." With that, Sheila waltzed out of the café.

"Now that you have the information you need, we'll be leaving. If you'll excuse us." Trevor gripped the mayor's elbow, and the older man went without argument.

The friend, Christopher, rose and paused next to her and Keith. "Debbie's a sweet girl. And very fortunate to have Nolan for a boss."

"I'm sure." Amy stared at the man's back as he exited the building. "Well, that was not what I expected."

Keith ran a hand over his face. "I really thought we'd ruffle the mayor's feathers, but instead, his response was calm. Insistent that Debbie's alive and well with her great-grandmother."

"What employer keeps a job open indefinitely?" Amy pivoted to face Keith. "You don't think he had an affair with Debbie, do you?"

"It would explain Sheila's icy exit. But I met

Nolan when I moved to Valley Springs a few years back, and if I had to make a statement about the man, it would be that he's loyal to a fault."

"Yeah, well, you never know what someone is capable of." Like lying and cheating on your best friend. Okay, so Keith hadn't cheated on her. It only felt that way. But still.

He opened his mouth then closed it.

Amy shouldn't have baited him, but she couldn't help herself. She mentally shook the thoughts from her mind. "How do you suppose the mayor got those texts if Debbie is dead? Or do we have it all wrong?"

"No, I'm 99 percent positive it's Debbie." Keith pulled his cell phone from his pocket and tapped the screen. "Something weird is going on. A dead woman can't text. I intend to find out who is impersonating our victim." He held the phone to his ear. "Jason, get me a warrant for Debbie Ackers's phone records and access to her GPS location." After a moment, Keith hung up. "My partner's on it."

"What's next for us?"

Hand shooting out to grip the back of the empty chair the mayor had occupied, Keith's shoulders slumped. Fatigue laced his features. "Not much we can do until we hear from Mel on the positive ID."

The strong, vibrant man she'd known most of

her life appeared ready to drop, but he'd never admit it. "Let's get out of here and regroup at your house. I could use a break. The events of the last couple of days are catching up with me."

A knowing lopsided grin greeted her words. "Then, by all means, let's go." He escorted her out the door and to his truck. Once inside his vehicle, he turned to her. "Thanks."

She splayed her hands out, palms up. "I have no idea what you're talking about."

Keith shook his head, then started the engine and pulled from the parking spot. On the short drive home, his eyes darted from the road to his mirrors.

Amy sensed the tension flowing from him. Her nerve endings sparked like live wires. "What's wrong?"

"Nothing."

"Don't give me that." She stopped herself from laying into him. He knew better than to keep her in the dark. She hated lies, even those by omission or under the pretense of protection.

The muscle in his jaw twitched. "I'm concerned that we poked the bear back at the café. If the mayor is our killer, he'll be out to stop us from continuing the investigation. Especially if he thinks you can identify him."

She bit her bottom lip and processed Keith's words. Replaying the conversation with the mayor in her mind, she recalled his actions. Things didn't add up. "I don't believe the mayor hurt Debbie. In fact, he seemed a little too caring about her."

"You may be right, but my gut says trouble is coming in a big way."

The truck stopped in front of Keith's house, and Amy scanned the surrounding woods before opening her door. If Keith's suspicions were correct, danger lurked nearby.

Had they made a mistake confronting the mayor and placed a bigger target on her back?

TEN

The burn in Keith's shoulder had intensified during his short outing. His body craved ibuprofen and rest. A nap was out of the question. He had too much to do. But taking a few minutes to unwind and let the medicine take effect was doable. He headed into the kitchen and grabbed the bottle of pain reliever and dropped two into his hand. Nope, he'd take the doctor's advice. He shook out a third and fourth tablet to join the other two. He swallowed the pills and prayed the prescription dosage took effect soon.

Ambling to the living room, he collapsed in the recliner, cradled his arm and closed his eyes. The hall clock ticked, and the bathroom door opened and closed. Quiet descended. He inhaled and allowed his body to relax.

No sooner than Amy's shower kicked on, cries emanated from the extra bedroom. Keith rubbed his eyes. *So, this is what it's like to be a parent.*

He traipsed up the stairs and peeked into the room Amy shared with Carter.

The baby's cry grew stronger.

"Hey, my man, what's wrong?" Keith scooped Carter from the portable crib, along with his stuffed elephant and blanket. His hand instantly discovered the problem. The little guy's diaper had leaked through and soaked his shirt and shorts. "I think we found what's causing the fuss. Didn't we?"

The baby's sobs eased as he stared at Keith. Carter lifted his chubby fingers and stuck them in Keith's mouth.

Keith chuckled. "Tell ya what, how about we take care of your diaper and clothes. Does that sound good?" He grabbed a diaper and new outfit then laid his son on the bedspread. "Can I tell you a secret?" The little boy kicked his legs. "I worry about your aunt—mom—aunt. We'll figure that out later. Anywho, I hope I can protect her. She means an awful lot to me, and I'm afraid I'm going to let her down."

His gaze drifted to the window. The sensation of eyes on him caused the hairs on the back of his neck to stand at attention. Was the killer out there ready to strike, or was Keith paranoid? He'd call Mel for an update on the autopsy once he finished with Carter. Hopefully, she'd identified the body, and he'd have confirmation that the remains were, in fact, Debbie's.

He undid the diaper. A foul odor filled the room. "Dude, that's disgusting."

Carter grinned and babbled to his stuffed elephant while Keith worked on cleaning up the mess.

He lifted the child onto his shoulder and took inventory of the bed, and sighed. "Well, I guess I need more practice." Keith chucked the diaper into the lidded waste can and turned back to the bedspread. What a mess, all over his mother's beautiful quilt. But he doubted she'd mind since it was her grandson. Pain gripped his heart. Another missing piece in his life. How he wished his mom could see her grandchild. He shook the thought from his mind and moved Carter to his sore shoulder. Scooping up the quilt and his son's dirty clothes, Keith headed for the laundry room.

No doubt, Amy's teasing jabs about his lack of ability weren't far off.

Steam filled the bathroom when Amy heard Carter's cries. She sighed and tightened the tie on the robe Keith had let her borrow. Before she slipped from the bathroom, the crying stopped. A smile curved on her lips. Carter must have fallen back asleep. Satisfied the infant no longer needed comfort, she turned back to the running water.

Ten minutes later, the hot shower had relaxed Amy's tense muscles and given her the break from reality she'd craved. The clean pair of shorts and tank top she now wore made her feel almost human again, and she ran a brush through her hair. Eyeing her makeup bag, she toyed with the idea of primping. She gave herself a mental slap. *He had a baby with your twin. Why on earth put yourself through more rejection?* Amy tucked the bag away and plodded to her room to check on Carter.

Light from the window seeped through the sheer curtains. The landscape beyond called to her. She tossed her dirty clothes on the rocking chair and tiptoed to the glass. Pulling back the lightweight material, she peered outside. Trees lined the road in the distance, and wildflowers dotting the field on the other side of Keith's fence line waved in the slight breeze. He'd found a beautiful property to set down roots of his own.

Pain tugged at her heart. She and Stacey had planned to live near each other. Even after her twin had joined the Army, Stacey had insisted that her home base always be within shouting distance. A sob clogged Amy's throat. She dropped the curtain, pivoted and bent to reclaim her laundry.

Glass shattered. An explosion boomed in the room.

Amy screamed and covered her head with her arms. Her ears rang. She peeked up. Fire danced across the bed and licked the ceiling.

Carter.

"No!" Orange-and-red flames blocked her path to his crib. Amy had to get to her baby.

She rushed toward the blaze, the heat searing her skin. The inferno consumed the portable crib. A sob tore from her throat. "Carter!"

Arms wrapped around her and pulled her away from her worst nightmare. "No! I have to save him!"

"It's okay, Ams."

"No, it's not!" Amy pushed away from Keith and dashed into the blazing room. A large hand gripped her wrist and yanked her to the hall. She stumbled and fell against his chest. "Let me go!"

Keith spun her to face him. "Carter's safe. He wasn't in there."

Wait, what? "He's okay?" She blinked the tears from her vision. "How?"

Ian rushed by with a fire extinguisher. "I called the fire department. Go to your little one and get out of here. I've got this."

Keith hurried her down the stairs away from the flames. "He woke while you were taking a shower. I changed him and brought him down to play with him."

Amy took two steps into the front room. Her gaze landed on a content Carter lying on the floor. Her legs turned to soggy noodles, and she collapsed against Keith. "My baby."

Sirens whined outside, and the slam of doors broke through her daze. Only then did she notice the smoky haze filling the room.

"Come on. VSFD is here. We need to get out of the house and let them do their job. Besides, if the fire gets out of control, I don't want you or Carter anywhere near the blaze." Keith scooped up Carter, laced his fingers with hers and tugged her toward the back door.

The warm, humid air smacked Amy in the face, stunning her out of her trance. Her gaze darted around the perimeter of Keith's property. "What if he sees us?"

Keith led her away from the house. "What are you talking about?"

She jerked him to a stop and stared at him. "The person who torched your house. What if he's still out here?"

Keith readjusted Carter to his shoulder and cupped her cheek. His blue-gray eyes held something she'd never witnessed in the man she'd grown up with. Fear. "The guys are on it. I promise we'll find him."

She knew he couldn't promise that, but she appreciated the sentiment. "When the projectile exploded through the window, the bed and curtains caught fire so fast I didn't have time to reach the crib." The words caught in her throat. "I thought…"

"Oh, Ams." Keith wrapped his arm around her and pulled her close. "I'm sorry you thought Carter…" His voice cracked. He pulled her against him. "Well, you know."

She laid her cheek on his chest. "I can't lose him. I just can't."

"And you won't. Not on my watch." Not letting go of her, Keith shuffled them to the fire trucks. "If someone is still out there, I want you out of sight." Tucking them between the two monster vehicles, he sat her on the metal step near the pump controls on one of the fire trucks. He shifted Carter into her arms and cupped her face. "Give yourself a minute. Then we can talk about what happened."

Amy inhaled Carter's baby scent. The simple action calmed her nerves.

Phone to his ear, Keith ran his fingers through his hair. "No, man, it wasn't an accident." Retelling the information, he paced the small area between the trucks, never going farther from her than a few yards. "This has got to stop. What if Carter had been sleeping in his crib?" He smacked the side of the fire truck with his palm. "My son would be dead!"

She jumped and snuggled Carter closer. Worry snaked in and wrapped around her. She'd never heard Keith yell before. In all the years she'd known him, he'd not once raised his voice in anger. She'd found it fascinating and endearing all wrapped into one.

His shoulders rose and fell. "Fine. Hurry up." Keith disconnected and exhaled. He crouched in front of her and placed his hand on the baby's back. "Sorry. Guess this shook me up more than I thought."

"I understand." And she did. The whole thing seemed surreal. One minute she became an aunt, and four short months later, she had a son and someone hunting her down to kill her.

Keith's blue eyes searched hers. "Yeah, I guess you do."

A throat cleared to her left.

Keith launched to his feet and positioned himself in front of her. When his shoulders drooped, Amy took a breath.

"Captain." Keith stepped toward the man and shook his hand. "I'd like you to meet Amy Baker. Amy, this is VSFD Captain Phillip Scott."

Captain Scott nodded. "Ma'am."

She stood on wobbly legs and shifted Carter to her left hip. "Nice to meet you, sir."

"Wish it was under better circumstances."

"Me, too."

Keith slipped his arm around Amy's waist and held tight. "What did you find?"

An arrow with a lead ball on the tip hung from the fire captain's gloved fingers. "Fire's out. Contained to the one bedroom, where we found this. I'm assuming from the way the glass shattered and the odor of lighter fluid on the arrow, this was the culprit that caused the fire."

Amy froze. All hope that she'd imagined the whole situation vanished. Someone had tried to eliminate her...again. And could very easily have killed Carter.

The open windows and fans in every room had cleared the majority of the smoke from the house. Keith had taken inventory of the damage and had already called the insurance company. The actions of his father and the firefighters had contained the damage to the single bedroom. Oh, how different the outcome could have been if he hadn't taken Carter downstairs or if Amy had taken a nap. The thoughts churned his stomach. His gaze traveled to the couch where Amy sat, snuggling Carter. He could have lost them both.

He spun and escaped to the kitchen for a moment to gather his swirling emotions. Placing his hands on the edge of the sink, he hung his head. The towering flames and Amy's screams played like a movie reel in his mind. Only by the grace of God had no one been hurt. "Thank You, Lord."

"Amen."

Keith tilted his head and found Dennis Monroe standing in the kitchen archway. "I… What if…" The words stuck in his throat. The thought of Amy or Carter caught in the fire immobilized him.

"No need to say it. I hear ya." His boss moseyed over and clapped him on his good shoulder. Leave it to Dennis to be aware of his injuries—both physical and emotional. "If you ever need to talk, you know where to find me." The man shrugged. "We scoured the area and came up empty. I have patrol outside monitoring the property until we meet as a group to discuss this, and then Doug will take over." Dennis waved his hand toward the living room. "Mel is here with the results of the autopsy. You up for going over the info?"

Was he? He hung his head and mustered the courage to face Amy. His lack of awareness had almost gotten her and Carter killed. Instead, she'd only suffered minor burns. Her face and arms had a pink color similar to a sunburn. The paramedics had recommended aloe when the burn ointment wore off. The incident could have been so much worse. God had looked out for all of them, Keith had no doubt. He lifted his tear-filled eyes to the ceiling and threw up another prayer of thanks.

After all that had happened in the short time since Amy had come into town, Keith should have anticipated an attack at the house. But no. He had lulled himself into a false sense of security on his own turf and with the guys patrolling the perimeter. He hadn't considered a long-distance assault. They'd only worried about someone sneaking into the house. He hadn't focused on an attack from beyond his property. The killer had waited until his father had moved to the opposite side of the house while on patrol. A mistake he refused to make again. He carried the burden of allowing the killer to strike on his watch. If he had to stay awake 24/7, he would if it meant protecting Amy and his son.

"Stop."

Straightening his spine, he pivoted to face Dennis. "What?"

"Stop blaming yourself. We all thought she'd be safe inside. This wasn't your fault."

Keith gaped at his boss. "How did you…"

"Let's say I've been there done that."

A flash of regret appeared then disappeared on Dennis's face so fast, Keith questioned whether or not he'd seen it. But the sheriff was right. He had to up his game and wallowing in his guilt wouldn't help. And not trusting his friends to do their jobs wasn't the answer either. He had to trust those around him and, ultimately, God to safeguard Amy.

The clomp of Dennis's boots echoed in the

kitchen as he went to the freezer and pulled out an ice pack and handed it to Keith. "Looks like you might need this."

The word *no* teetered on his lips, but Keith knew it would be a lie. "Thanks." He slid his arm back into the sling, took the pack and held it to his shoulder. He'd asked his friend Ethan, one of the paramedics, to rewrap his shoulder after the man had attended to Amy's burns. His muscles were on fire, and the ache persisted with a vengeance, but a few more days and he'd be able to ditch the sling completely.

Dennis jerked his head toward the living room. "Come on. Let's see what Mel has to say."

When they walked into the living room, a lump formed in Keith's throat. Amy sat in the recliner with Carter in her arms. His dad, Jason, Mel, along with Kyle and Doug, had come to support him and Amy. The eyes of the group landed on him. "I...um..." He swallowed hard.

"Thanks for letting us crash here instead of the station." Mel scooted closer to Amy and gave Carter her finger to tug on. "I, for one, wanted more time seeing this son of yours. Isn't that right, Carter?"

Thank you, Melanie. Last year, when Mel had returned to town after ten years, she'd fit right into the group. At least after she and Jason patched up an old hurt.

Keith cleared his throat. "I'm glad you all stopped by. I really appreciate it."

Jason propped his ankle on his knee and stretched his arm across the back of the couch. "We've got your back, bro. Don't ever forget that."

An emotional reaction took Keith by surprise. He scanned the group. They'd dropped everything and pitched in. Doug and Kyle had covered the broken window with plywood, while Jason and Dennis had carried the charred mattress and bed frame from the house and loaded it in Keith's truck. Someone, he wasn't sure who, had cut the carpet out and had added it to the pile of mangled objects to go to the dump. His father had called a contractor and set up an appointment for the reconstruction that needed to be done. Keith calling the insurance company seemed like a minor job compared to what the others had accomplished.

He blinked back the moisture from his eyes. He had great friends.

Stuff. That's all. Everything was replaceable. But he had to admit, he was thankful that he'd put his mother's favorite quilt in the washer. His heart ached at the idea of losing a piece of his mother so soon after she'd passed away. He shook off the thought. All things considered, he hadn't lost much. The only casualty was the old rocking chair that his grandmother had passed down to his mother. But with a little sanding and stain, the family heirloom would look like new.

Hand resting on his sidearm, Doug nodded at Keith and waltzed to the front door. "My turn to walk the perimeter." He pointed his glare at Kyle. "Don't forget to relieve me."

Kyle grinned and feigned a look of innocence. "Who me?"

"That's what I thought. Well, if you're going to leave me outside, at least do something useful." Doug rolled his eyes and slipped from the house.

How would he ever repay his friends for all they had done for him?

Kyle rubbed his hands together, looking like a shark ready for a meal. "If Mel would quit playing with the baby, maybe we could solve this case."

Melanie stuck her tongue out at Kyle. "Whatever." She extracted her finger from Carter's grip and grabbed the file off the coffee table. Sliding back against the couch cushion, she flipped open the document. "I have a positive ID on the victim. It is, without a doubt, Debbie Ackers."

Kyle whistled. "Not that it was unexpected, but where does that leave Mayor Taylor?"

"Either he's lying, or someone is playing him." Keith took the chair Dennis brought from the kitchen and sat it next to Amy. He couldn't help himself. The urge to be next to her outweighed his common sense. He slung the ice pack over his left shoulder and placed his right hand on Carter's back. Is this what it felt like to be a dad? The need to touch his son, confirming the little guy was safe. That same stupid lump formed in his throat. The baby in Amy's arms had turned his emotions into mushy jelly.

As if Amy had read Keith's mind, she plucked the ice pack from his shoulder and shifted Carter into his arms. He snuggled the baby and inhaled the fresh baby shampoo scent. That did it. All the stress and fear from today smothered him, making it hard to breathe. Tears blurred his eyes. He blinked, hoping no one had noticed.

Amy's lopsided smile told him she hadn't missed the glaze of moisture.

"What do y'all think? Is the mayor telling the truth?" Kyle's question brought Keith back to the conversation.

"He seemed to believe what he said." Keith kissed Carter's head then laid his cheek on the boy's soft hair. "What was your impression, Ams?"

She tucked her hands under her thighs. "I think he believes that Debbie's been sending him messages. But…" Amy hesitated.

Keith shifted to face her. "But what?"

"It's nothing." She dipped her face, hiding her expression.

He placed his finger under her chin and lifted. "No. Go ahead. Say what you're thinking."

She exhaled. "He's hiding something. I'm just not sure it's Debbie's demise." Amy scooped up her hair and used the black band on her wrist to secure it into a ponytail. "If you look at it through a wide lens, his responses ring true, but there's something blurry on the fringe of the picture."

"Couldn't help yourself, could you?" Keith chuckled. Amy's love for photography tended to come out in her speech.

"Sorry. Occupational hazard." The tiny dimple appeared on her cheek. The one that sent Keith's heart racing.

How had he messed things up so badly? If he could go back and make different choices, he would. But then he wouldn't have the sweet baby in his arms.

"Any idea what he's hiding?" Jason twirled a strand of his wife's hair.

Amy shook her head. "Not a clue." Her gaze landed on Keith.

He shrugged. He agreed with Amy; the mayor's behavior was off, but he had no idea why. This was the hardest part of an investigation—the part where you were unable to find a thread to pull to unravel the entire mystery.

Dennis cleared his throat. "Let's not focus on what we can't figure out but look at what we know." The sheriff stuffed his hands in his jeans pockets and shifted his attention to Melanie. "What else do you have, Mel?"

The county's newly acquired coroner scooted to the edge of the couch and placed the open file on the coffee table. "A few hairs were found on the victim, but without a hair follicle, I can't get DNA. The lab is analyzing the strands for anything that might be useful, but it will take a while."

"No chance it's Debbie's?" Keith rubbed Carter's back. The baby snuggled in and sucked on his fist.

Melanie shook her head. "Debbie had auburn hair. The pieces found were brown. No red tint at all."

"Well, that narrows it down." Jason rolled his eyes. "Brown isn't exactly rare."

"Leave it to my partner to point out the obvious." Keith glanced at Amy.

Bags had come to reside under her eyes. The bruises on her face had darkened. Quite a contrast to the paleness that had appeared after the fire. She fidgeted with the hem of her shirt, almost as if trying to occupy her hands.

Keith shifted, careful of his healing injury, and placed his son back in Amy's arms.

Her eyes widened at his gesture.

A quick nod earned him a slight smile. Even

after all these years and the tension between them, they could read each other's thoughts. Maybe not everything had changed between them. The idea gave him a glimmer of hope.

Amy rested the baby on her chest and buried her face in his soft peach fuzz hair. He noticed that the tension in her shoulders released.

Keith settled back against his chair, missing the warmth of his son's body.

Jason leaned forward and reached over Mel's shoulder. "What else ya got?"

Melanie slapped his hand and glared at him. "Paws off."

Keith chuckled at his partner's antics.

"Anywho," Mel began. "I found a piece of blue-tinted plastic near the body. But you have to remember that if anything landed more than four feet from the victim, it most likely was sucked into the lake by the waves."

"Do you have any ideas what the plastic is from?" Dennis asked.

Melanie shook her head. "Not happening. It would be purely a guess. But the lab rats are on it." The good doctor had tagged her lab assistants with the moniker not long after she'd arrived. Daniel and Jen insisted they hated the term, but both swelled with pride anytime Mel called them that.

"Let me know what they discover." The sheriff

snagged a chair from the kitchen and straddled it backward.

"When I know, you'll know." Mel relaxed back against Jason. "That's all I have. You have to remember, Debbie's been down there a long time. Whatever evidence the killer left, the elements took care of it. It's gone."

Keith noticed the strain in Melanie's features; the woman hated loose ends. He shifted to lean forward. A spasm in his shoulder shot through him. He gritted his teeth and eased back onto his chair. "We'll take what we can get, Mel. Have you found any evidence connecting Debbie's killer to either Stacey or Detective Jefferies?"

"Not as of yet. I focused on identifying the body, but I've pulled the case files for the other two. I'll dive in tomorrow and see if anything jumps out at me."

"Did you—" Amy's voice caught. "Did you perform my sister's autopsy?" Amy's face paled beneath the pink from her burns.

Compassion flowed from Melanie. She placed her hand on Amy's knee. "Yes, I did. I took good care of her."

"Thank you. I'm glad it was you." A tear leaked out and trickled down Amy's cheek.

The interaction between the two women left Keith aching for Amy's loss of her sister. The two might have clashed, but they'd had a special bond even beyond that of twins. He scanned the room looking anywhere but at Amy. The guys had averted their gazes and found other focal points away from the touching moment.

"I know it's cliché, but Stacey died instantly from the gunshot wound. Other than the initial car crash, she didn't suffer. She was gone before he tried to torch the car. I hope that helps." Mel wiped at the moisture building on her lashes.

"It does," Amy squeaked out. She buried her face in the crook of Carter's neck. Her shoulders shook.

Her silent sobs shattered Keith's heart. He had no choice but to wrap her in his arms and hold her while she mourned the death of her twin.

The tick of the grandfather clock standing in the entry echoed through the silent room. Keith's friends stared at him and Amy. The hum of the ceiling fans and the whine of cicadas floated through the open windows and added to the rhythmic tick-tock. A faint smell of smoke still lingered in the air.

Keith eased back and grabbed a handful of tissues. He pushed them into Amy's hand.

She mopped up her tears. "Sorry about that."

"Ams, you have nothing to be sorry for." His fingers brushed the damp hair from her temples. "It's okay."

Inhaling a big cleansing breath, Amy pulled herself together. "Let's keep going."

Keith studied her. "If you're sure. We can put the conversation on hold a little longer if you need time."

"No, I'm okay," she responded, but the room remained quiet for several minutes.

Kyle pushed off the wall and slipped to the floor, resting his back against the kitchen door-jamb. "So. Who are we considering players in this twisted crime? We have the mayor, but who else are you guys thinking needs to be on that list?"

Amy ran her knuckles over Carter's cheek. "His son, Trevor, had a bit of an attitude and didn't want us talking to his father."

"Don't forget his friend Christopher. The man never looked up from his plate. And I can't figure out Sheila, his wife. She couldn't have cared less. Just had to get to her next appointment." Keith rubbed his forehead. "The whole group seemed odd."

Screams pierced the air.

"Hey!" Doug's deep voice filtered through the open windows.

Keith braced his sore arm and bolted from his seat, following Dennis, Jason and Melanie to the door. He pivoted, his eyes connecting with Amy's. "Stay with Dad." He hurried outside. Keith had let his guard down earlier in the day, and a fire had come close to taking the woman he cared for—a lot—and his son from him. He refused to let it happen again. He had to get his act together, or his ineptness would cost Amy her life.

Carter on her hip, Amy paced the living room. Within minutes, she'd received a text message from Keith referring to some sort of accident, but he hadn't gone into detail.

The hint of smoke tickled her nose, reminding her of the sinking feeling she'd experienced when the fire had taken hold and she'd thought Carter was in his crib. Amy swallowed the bile creeping up her throat and shoved the memory down.

Voices floated through the window. Amy's gaze drifted to the opening. Had the killer gotten close again?

A nagging headache gripped her temples from her crying jag. She hated that she'd lost it in front of everyone. However, there was something cathartic about the release. And knowing Melanie had been the one who'd taken care of Stacey gave Amy a sense of comfort.

"Come on, honey. Have a seat." Ian patted the sofa next to him.

No way could she sit while the others were outside, possibly in danger. "What do you think is taking so long?" Only five minutes had passed, and she made it sound like they'd left hours ago.

"That my boy and his friends are well trained. They'll be fine. You need to relax, or you'll worry my grandson."

Ian had a point. Carter's spine had stiffened, and tiny whimpers met her ears. "Sorry, little guy." She rolled her neck and glanced at the window. No gunshots. No more screams. Only muffled voices drifted through the screen. She had to get out there and see for herself that everything was okay.

Amy strode to Ian and placed his grandson in his arms. She leaned down and kissed the baby. "Please take good care of him."

"Amy."

She ignored Ian's plea and strode to the front porch. For her sanity, she had to find out what happened.

Arms wrapped around her waist, she descended the steps. She spied a group of people crowded at the end of the short lane. She hurried toward the commotion. "Keith."

He spun. Amy knew the exact moment he spotted her. His shoulders tensed. "Ams. What are you doing out here?" Gravel crunched under his boots. "I want you inside."

"And I want to know what's going on." She straightened her spine, pretending to have more courage than she did.

He sighed. "All right. Come on. But stick close to me."

She fell into step beside him. No problem on her part. Amy might appear brave, but her stomach had knotted. Her attacker had failed multiple times, but she couldn't count on his unsuccessful attempts on her life indefinitely. It was only a matter of time before she ended up on the cold hard steel table in Melanie's lab, unless Keith and his friends arrested the man responsible for the string of bodies in her wake.

Her eyes adjusted to the dim light of the evening. Amy gasped. "What happened?"

A young girl, maybe thirteen or fourteen, sat on the ground holding her arm while Melanie knelt next to her, examining the injury. An older boy stood near, face full of shock.

"That's what we're trying to find out, but we're having a little trouble. Mel's tending to Becky's injuries, and Zeke is a bit shaken. Neither have settled down enough to give us a full picture yet. All we can get from them is that someone hit Becky's bike." Keith placed his hand on the small of Amy's back and motioned to the teens. The warmth of his touch stirred feelings she'd rather not experience.

"Okay, Zeke. Let's try this again." Jason crouched to the kid's level. "Start from the beginning."

"We…" The boy cleared his throat. "Mom sent

us to the store to grab a gallon of milk." The young man's gaze shifted to the girl.

Keith moved next to Amy's ear. "This is Becky and Zeke from down the road." He nodded to the boy, encouraging Zeke to continue.

"A truck sat right over there." Zeke pointed to a small turnout a little way down the road. The spot was hidden between bushes on either side. "When we rode by, we waved at the driver."

Keith tensed beside her. "What color was the vehicle?"

"Kind of an old green."

"You said you waved. Did you recognize the driver?"

Amy held her breath, praying that the young man identified her attacker.

"No. Just being friendly, that's all."

Her hope deflated. *God, when will we catch a break? I want to be free from all this, and I want justice for my sister.*

"What happened next?" Jason's question broke through Amy's despair.

"The engine revved, and the truck headed straight for us. I steered my bike into the ditch, but Becky got clipped." The teen's voice wobbled. "I'm supposed to watch out for her."

Amy's heart hurt for the young man. He obviously felt responsible. She could relate. Stacey's death had been her fault. Still, the boy couldn't have stopped the driver from hitting his sister. "Zeke, you aren't responsible for someone else's choices."

Keith raised a brow and smiled. "Listen to her, Zeke, my man."

"But Mom told me to keep Becky safe." Tears glistened in the young man's eyes.

"Your mom will understand." Jason gently slapped the boy's back.

The kid lowered his gaze and toed the gravel with his tennis shoe. "I hope so."

"Thanks for your help," Keith added.

"Sure." Zeke returned his attention to his sister and knelt beside her.

With a tug on Amy's sleeve, Keith pulled her away from the group. "I think Becky and Zeke saved us from another attack."

Amy wasn't sure about anything right now. Had the teens experienced an unfortunate event, or had they scared away the killer? "You really think so?"

"I do." Keith swung his head from side to side. "Valley Springs is a small town, and I know most of the people who live here, but I have no clue who owns a truck like that."

She dropped her head in her hands. "I don't know what to do. Stacey's dead, and so is Trent. And now, Becky's hurt. It could have been so much worse."

Keith removed her hands from her face and tipped up her chin with his index finger. "But it wasn't."

She blinked back the tears threatening to fall. "I can't bear the thought of someone else injured or dying because of me. Who else has to lose their life before he finds and kills me?"

"I won't let that happen."

His soft words gave her hope. But then again... "What if you can't stop it?"

Keith's jaw twitched. "I lost Stacey. I won't lose you, too."

The words pierced her heart. For a brief moment, she'd thought Keith had more than friendly feelings for her. She lost her focus on the path, and her toe hit a rock. She stumbled and dropped to the ground. The sharp gravel dug into her skin through her jeans. How stupid could she get? Thinking that Keith might be interested in her.

"Careful, Ams." Keith's words broke through her haze.

She shook her head. "I'm okay."

"Pardon me for saying so, but you don't look okay." He gripped her shoulders and gave her hands and knees a once-over. "The ambulance just arrived. Let me get one of the paramedics."

The siren and flashing blue lights registered in her brain. "No. It's only scrapes and scratches. Becky needs them more than I do."

Keith nodded but didn't look convinced.

She cupped his face with her hand. "Relax, cowboy. I tripped. Nothing more than a slight sting." *Liar.* Her hands and knees ached, along with her heart. She gazed into the depths of his blue-gray eyes and wished things could be different. She wanted to be the twin he dreamed about, the twin he chose.

For the longest moment, he crouched beside her, not saying a word. A large sigh filled the space between them. "If you're sure." He held out his hands. "You think you can get up?"

She nodded and accepted his offer. The simple touch sent butterflies fluttering in her stomach. Not quick enough to contain her surprise, a gasp fell from her lips. Amy stared at his hands.

"Ams." Keith gripped her fingers tighter. His eyes darkened.

A throat cleared, breaking the moment between them. "Sorry to interrupt."

Not letting go nor looking at his partner, Keith maintained eye contact with her. "What's up, Jason?"

"Just wanted to tell you that I've got this. I'll take Zeke and Becky's official statement and make sure their mom gets here. Why don't you take Amy inside and check on Carter?"

"Thanks, man. I appreciate it." Keith hadn't moved—his focus remained completely on her.

Had he felt the attraction? The same yearning she had?

Amy was being ridiculous. He'd chosen Stacey. Her nephew was all the proof she needed. Yet, his lingering touch said differently.

He led her to the house and opened the door.

She stepped inside, itching to grab Carter, bury her face against his soft skin and inhale his sweet baby smell. The one thing that always calmed her and cleared her head. But she didn't move when she noticed Keith scanning the perimeter of his property.

Her attacker was still out there somewhere, waiting for the perfect moment to make his move. She sent up a silent prayer for Keith's safety. Without a doubt, Keith would put himself in the line of fire in his attempt to find the person responsible for all the death and torment that had followed Amy for the past four months.

Keith ushered her into the house. "Come on. Let's get you out of sight."

"Is someone…"

"Not that I know of, but I'm not taking chances." His gaze drifted to Carter. The corner of his mouth lifted then dropped. "What if I hadn't taken him out of the bedroom?"

Amy understood his concern. Her heart pounded at the memory of thinking her son was in the crib when the fire started. She sucked in a shaky breath, lifted Carter from his grandpa's arms and kissed the baby's chubby little cheek. She pivoted and handed Carter to Keith. "God knew and provided for his escape from danger. You."

Keith shifted the baby's weight away from his sore shoulder. He dropped his face into the crook of Carter's neck and inhaled a shuddering breath.

The sight of father and son had Amy blinking back tears. "I guess I should make a little area out here for a makeshift crib."

"You and Carter—" Keith lifted his head and cleared the emotion from his throat "—can take my room. I'll crash on the couch."

"We'll be fine out here."

"No. I don't want you that close to the front door. I'll feel better if you take my bedroom."

In all honesty, she'd feel safer away from the door and downstairs windows. Of course, that hadn't helped earlier. "All right. I'll go to the kitchen and look through the things that your friends salvaged from the bedroom." She rubbed her hand down Carter's back and forced herself to leave him in his father's capable hands.

A pile of washed clothes and cleaned odds and ends sat on the kitchen table. The crew there earlier had taken care of sorting through the things from her room and either washing or tossing depending on the status of each object. Someone, most likely Melanie, had even run to the store to purchase more diapers. Amy peered into a small basket and smiled. New rattles and teethers lay in there, ready for use. She'd have to figure out a way to thank Keith's friends—friends who had quickly become hers, as well.

Amy rummaged through the items and found pajamas and clothes for tomorrow. She scanned the remaining items. Her eyes landed on the rocking chair in the corner by the back door. She ambled to the piece of furniture and ran her hand down the scorched wood.

The reality of what had happened crashed around her. If she hadn't bent down, the flaming arrow would have hit her straight on. And if Keith hadn't taken Carter downstairs, she and her baby would both be dead.

ELEVEN

Keith tagged last night as the longest night ever.

He'd helped Amy settle into his room, then grabbed a pillow and blanket and stretched out on the couch. His father had excused himself moments later, as if he'd known Keith needed alone time to process the day's events. But how did someone process almost losing his best friend and son in one fiery moment?

After tossing and turning for half the night in an attempt to get comfortable, Keith had switched to the recliner to relieve pressure on his shoulder. He'd dozed on and off for a few hours and finally gave up when the sun peeked through the blinds.

Coffee mug in hand and eggs and sausage staying warm in the oven for when the rest of the house woke up, Keith slipped onto a kitchen chair. Elbows on the table, he sipped the dark brew and closed his eyes, inhaling the hazelnut aroma from his special stash. He required the extra jolt today. Between the soreness in his arm, the vivid images of the flames licking the ceiling and Amy's guttural cry for Carter, his head ached.

Cute babbling filtered in from the living room. Keith smiled and pushed the throbbing in his temples to the back of his mind. He still had a difficult time believing he had a son.

Carter on her hip, Amy stepped through the doorway. "You're up early."

Her sleep-mussed hair made Keith's stomach flip. Even in her sleepy state, Amy was the most gorgeous woman he'd ever known. Identical twin aside, there was something about her that Stacey hadn't possessed. A softness in Amy's features mixed with a determination that rivaled a world-class athlete's... She was incredible. Amy made his heart flutter like no other woman ever had. He gave his head a shake, dislodging the direction of his thoughts. She deserved a better man than him. Granted, his poor choices happened before he'd met God, but he hadn't trusted Amy with the truth, and now it hung between them.

Keith scooted from the table and stood. "Yup. Coffee's fresh, and breakfast is in the oven. Would you like some?"

"Sounds great." Amy prepared a bottle for Carter and cradled him in the crook of her arm. Within seconds loud slurping filled the kitchen.

Keith chuckled while he prepared her plate. "He really enjoys his meals." He placed the food and a cup of coffee next to Amy. "There ya go."

She juggled feeding a baby and eating her breakfast like a pro. Something Keith had yet to learn. He'd had a crash course in diaper changing and bathing the little guy, along with learning how to work the portable crib. He'd also become an expert at buckling and unbuckling the contraption called a car seat, but the ability to do two things at once continued to elude him.

Fork halfway to her mouth, Amy's dimple deepened. "Thank you for breakfast."

He smiled and flicked his fingers at her. "Keep eating. But you're welcome." He refilled his drink and waltzed back to the table.

"So, what are the plans for today?" she asked around bites.

Slipping onto his seat again with a fresh cup of joe, he leaned forward. Fingers wrapped around his mug, he watched his son. The kid was amazing. Of course, he could be a biased father. Keith flopped against the back of his chair. A father. Apparently, his brain hadn't come to grips with the fact yet.

"You okay?" Amy lifted Carter to her shoulder and patted his back.

"Yup." Keith blinked away the lingering shock. "I talked with the sheriff early this morning. He agreed to let me continue investigating, but I have to keep Jason in the loop since he's the lead detective on this." He snorted. "I think Dennis knows it's a lost cause to tell me no. So, with the sheriff's blessing, we'll go see the mayor. Tell him about Mel identifying Debbie's body and watch his reaction."

"You still think he's lying, don't you?"

Keith shrugged. "I'm not sure. Seems convenient, but who knows. The other day his responses seemed genuine." Either that or the man could convincingly lie at will.

"Well, you can't have it both ways. You either believe him or not." She mopped up Carter's face with the burp cloth she had on her shoulder.

"True." Keith ran his fingers through his hair. "Guess I want a second look."

Amy stood and handed Carter to him. "Here. Take your son while I get ready."

Carter's chubby hands pushed on Keith's chest. The little man leaned back and gave him a big toothless grin. "Aren't you a happy one." How did one little baby turn a grown man's insides to mush?

Once Amy finished getting ready, Keith handed Carter over to his father's care.

"Bye, sweetie." Amy gave the infant one last squeeze.

"Let's go see what Mayor Taylor has to say."

Keith escorted her to his truck and slipped in behind the wheel.

Amy scanned the area.

"Please try not to worry. Kyle patrolled this morning. He left about twenty minutes ago."

"Your friends have been amazing helping out during their off-hours. I don't know how I'll ever repay them." She twisted her hands in her lap.

He flipped the blinker on and turned the corner. "They are great. And I don't think you need to worry about repaying them. That's what small towns do. They help each other. They want you and Carter safe."

She nodded and gazed out the passenger window.

A quick glance at Amy and his heart stuttered. What would he do if something happened to her or Carter? He had to find the person responsible for Stacey's death and the attempts on Amy's life. He owed it to Stacey for his gigantic blunder, and he owed it to Amy for losing her trust in him. And most of all, Carter. His son shouldn't grow up without a mother.

The town square bustled with activity. A car pulled out from in front of City Hall, and Keith thanked God for the closeness to the main entrance.

"Stay put." He put the truck into Park and hurried to the passenger side. "Okay, let's do this."

Amy slid from the seat. Worry etched her

features. "You really think I'm in danger while standing in the middle of town?"

"I'm not taking any chances." He wrapped his arm around her waist and escorted her upstairs to the mayor's office.

Keith pushed open the glass door that read *Mayor Nolan Taylor* and followed Amy inside.

The contemporary design of the waiting room contradicted the mayor's good ol' country boy image. Keith supposed being a political figure even in a small town required a bit of couth.

"Good morning, Detective." The mayor's new receptionist—according to her nameplate, Heather—greeted him.

Keith wondered if Nolan had hired the woman on a temporary basis or knew Debbie wasn't returning and hired Heather permanently. He was dying to ask but refrained. He wanted to see the mayor's reaction to the information and not tip his hand prematurely.

"Good morning, Heather. Is the mayor in? I need to speak with him about Debbie Ackers."

The comment didn't faze the woman. She placed a call to her boss then motioned them to go on into the mayor's inner office.

A shiver zipped up Amy's spine as she entered the mayor's private workspace. She wrapped her arms around her waist, warding off the sensation of impending doom. Was this the man who had killed Debbie and Amy's sister and intended on killing her, too? She hadn't thought so, but the question lingered in her mind.

"Welcome." Mayor Taylor shook Keith's hand and nodded to her. He gestured to the two seats in front of his desk and lowered himself into his plush office chair. "What can I help you with?"

Amy's stomach churned. Nervous energy had her visually exploring the room.

Keith sat and leaned forward, forearms on his knees. "We came to inform you that the coroner's office identified the body beneath the cliff."

The mayor's gaze never left Keith's. "Who was it?"

Amy pivoted to watch the man's reaction as Keith delivered the information.

"Debbie Ackers."

The mayor sucked in a breath. His face paled, and he collapsed against his seat. "I—It can't be. She texted me yesterday."

Keith raised an eyebrow. "What did she say?"

"That she's moving in with her grandmother and wouldn't be back." The mayor's shoulders slumped. "It wasn't her, was it?"

Amy almost snorted. *Ya think?* She bit the inside of her cheek to hold back the snark. The antsiness swirling within her had her on edge.

"No, sir, it's not."

Taylor ran a hand down his face. "I..." His voice cracked. "I don't understand why someone is pretending to be her."

"Whoever texted you wanted you to think she was alive."

"But why?" The mayor's perplexed expression had Amy going with her initial assessment that he wasn't involved. The man looked shocked. No, that wasn't right either. He looked nauseous. Why on earth had the news affected him in such a way? He might not have killed Debbie, but the man was holding something back.

"Now, that's a question I want an answer to." Keith sat up straight.

The mayor's Adam's apple bobbed. "So, you believe me?"

"I must admit, I'm not one hundred percent convinced. But I am leaning that way."

The air whooshed from Taylor's lungs. He leveled his gaze at a picture on his desk that included Debbie and pinched the bridge of his nose.

Amy studied the image that had captured Taylor's attention and pulled her phone from her pocket. She pretended to check her messages while she took a snapshot. She casually turned and perused the pictures on the wall. Photo after photo lined the interior of the office. Hunting pictures of him, his son and his best friend, Christopher. One with their rifles slung over their shoulders and a beautiful twelve-point buck in front of them. An obviously successful day.

She stepped to the next frame. The same three posed with compound bows proudly held in front of them. Another photo caught Amy's eye. One of the mayor and his wife, Sheila, both decked out in camo. The entire family seemed to be in on the sport of hunting in some way. However, Sheila looked a bit out of place with her full face of makeup and perfectly manicured nails. Amy lifted her phone and quietly snapped several pictures of the images on the wall.

Tucking her phone into her pocket, Amy tapped the frame of one of the photos. "You're quite the hunter." The memory of the flaming arrow exploding through the bedroom window replayed like a five-second GIF over and over. Her heart pounded. The smoke so real she could taste it. She shook the nightmare from her brain.

The mayor blinked. "Excuse me?"

"Hunting. You like to hunt."

"Yes. My father taught me, and I taught my son. We spend many weekends a year together as a family at our cabin." Taylor rose, sauntered over and stood next to her.

If the man had killed someone, he was a great actor. Still, the possibility he might have killed three people so far had the hair on her arms prickling.

Taylor traced his finger over one of the photos. "Family is important to me. I…um… Thank you for letting me know about Debbie. I still can't believe I've been duped this whole time." The mayor shifted to face Keith. "Is there anything else, Detective?"

"Yes, could you please send me the contact information for Debbie's family? We'll need to notify them of her death."

The mayor swatted the air. "Of course, of course. I'll have my administrative assistant send it to you as soon as we finish up here."

"Thank you, sir." Keith stood and moved toward the door.

Amy joined him, ready to get out of the enclosed space with a possible murderer.

"Please let me know what you find out." A flash of sorrow crossed Taylor's face then cleared. "Thank you for stopping by."

She and Keith exited at the obvious dismissal.

Keith's hand warmed the small of her back. The tightness in her chest eased. She'd always felt safe with him, and today was no different. The past year had left scars on her heart, but she knew without a doubt she could trust him with her and Carter's lives.

"I—"

Keith narrowed his gaze and shook his head. His warning stopped the question from leaving her lips. Either Keith didn't believe the mayor had told the truth, or he worried about listening ears. Someone else nearby watching—waiting. Panic crawled up her throat.

Leaning in, Keith whispered, "Breathe, honey. Breathe."

"What if…what if he isn't the one? What if someone else…"

"I'm not going to let anything happen to you." He wrapped his arms around her and held her close.

"Promise?"

He remained quiet.

Of course, he couldn't promise. Amy knew he'd do his best, but it was only a matter of time if they didn't catch her attacker soon.

TWELVE

Stretching out his legs, Keith folded his hands over his stomach. Jason and Melanie had stopped by to hear about his and Amy's trip to the mayor's office and go over the case. "I think I believe him."

Jason straddled the chair he'd dragged in from the kitchen and rested his arms on the top rung. "Well, that's an exact science."

Keith pursed his lips together. "Knock it off."

"Just saying." His partner smirked.

"Anywho. Mayor Taylor's reaction was too instantaneous to be fake."

"I trust your instincts, man. But I'd like more than your gut. I asked Doug to check out Nolan's alibi for the events that we have exact dates and times for. If the mayor isn't our killer, that will prove it. Doesn't mean he didn't hire it done, though."

"That's true. I asked Kyle to dig into Debbie's background. See if someone from her past has a grudge against her."

"Did he find anything interesting?"

"Nope. Her mom died a few years ago, and she moved to Valley Springs not long after. A couple of boyfriends, but one is happily married now, and the split with the other seemed mutual, according to friends. There's nothing that sends up a red flag." Keith felt secure with the details Kyle reported on the background check. The man was nothing but thorough.

"If Kyle says there's nothing there, then I believe him. I've known Debbie for a while. She's not the type to have enemies. She was a quiet young lady who always went out of her way to help others." Jason drummed his fingers on the chair. "And that, my friend, brings us back to the short list of possible suspects." Melanie walked in, and Jason peered up at his wife and smiled.

The two had mended fences and hadn't wasted time getting married. Keith envied his partner. Keith's dream of a wife and family seemed further away every day. Correction. Wife. He had a son. His gaze landed on Amy and Carter. If he hadn't messed up with her twin, maybe he and Amy would be dating now and on their way to a permanent relationship. His son meant the world to him, and even though he had regrets, Carter would never be one of them.

"What do you think, Amy? I'm all about the detective prowess of these two handsome gentlemen, but I want a woman's intuition." Melanie handed Jason a glass of tea, then lowered herself to the floor and crisscrossed her legs. She took a sip of her drink and set it on the coffee table.

Amy rocked Carter in the recliner and appeared to consider her words before speaking. "I have to agree with Keith. The mayor seemed genuinely surprised. But…" She chewed on her bottom lip.

Keith met her gaze. What had she noticed? "But what? Go ahead. What are you thinking?"

"I still say he's hiding something. I have no idea what, but the man is holding back. He became guarded every time we mentioned Debbie's name. Same as at the diner."

"So, he didn't kill her, but he knows something about it?" Jason lowered his chin to his forearms.

Amy shook her head. "No. I don't think so. It's like he's trying to hide a secret."

"What kind of secret?" Melanie shifted to look at Amy. "Do you think he was having an affair with her?"

"Maybe." Amy laid her head against Carter's. "I'm not sure. I only know that something felt off."

"Well, there's a rumor about the man having an affair. So, it's possible, I guess. I say we dig a little deeper into Nolan beyond an alibi, but if that comes back clean, then let's take him off the list as a murder suspect," Jason clarified.

Keith mulled over the comment and nodded. "I'll have Kyle continue looking into Debbie's past. But yes. I think that's the way to go."

Melanie flipped open the folder she'd brought with her. "If we take him out of the running for killer, that leaves us with Nolan's son, Trevor, and his friend Christopher, unless Kyle uncovers someone else." Melanie tapped the paper. "Would either be able to use a bow to make that shot with the arrow into Amy's room?"

"Definitely. From the pictures I saw in the mayor's office, the three of them are expert hunters. Rifle, crossbow, you name it, they appear to be skilled." Amy patted Carter's back while the baby sucked on his pacifier, sound asleep in her arms.

Keith itched to hold Amy. The trip to City Hall had taken its toll on her. She was a strong woman, but who wouldn't be at a breaking point under these circumstances? His heart tripped over itself at the lines of fatigue etching her features.

"What about Nolan's wife, Sheila?" Jason asked. "If the mayor had an affair with Debbie, she'd have motive."

"Not sure about that one." Keith scratched his chin. "If the affair happened and she found out, Sheila's the type to get revenge. But from what I know about her, she doesn't like to get her hands dirty. Literally."

Melanie traced the path of the water droplets down the side of her glass. "That may be true, but it's worth considering. My aunt hated working in the dirt, but man, was she a crack shot."

"You have a point, Mel. It's possible." Keith rubbed the back of his neck. "I'll add it to the list and talk to Dennis about it tomorrow."

"And don't forget. More than one person is involved." Amy stopped rocking. "Someone broke into my home at the same time shots were fired at Trent."

Keith nodded. "You're right." The whole situation was a tangled mess of cases. "And let's not dismiss the fact that Eagle Bay PD never sent the sheriff's department Amy's report about the shooting on the cliff. I have Doug taking a closer look into that."

"So, EBPD has a dirty cop?" Jason scowled.

"Doesn't have to be a cop, sweetie." Mel patted her husband's knee. "Think about everyone that works at the station. Could be anyone from the receptionist to the tech guru."

Keith cringed. "Thanks a lot, Mel. You just gave me a headache."

She lifted her glass in salute. "I aim to please."

"Now what?" Amy's gaze darted around the room from person to person.

"Now we do a deep dive into all our players. No one is exempt." Keith shifted and winced. His shoulder no longer had a constant ache, but it reminded him of the injury when he moved wrong.

Jason checked his watch and rose. "I'm heading out to relieve Kyle on patrol for a few hours."

"And I'm going home. I'll look over the autopsy reports of Debbie, Stacey and Trent again and see if anything pops out at me." Melanie joined her husband at the door.

"I can't thank you enough for the help." Keith stood.

"That's what friends are for." Jason escorted Melanie out the door, and Keith closed it behind them.

He spun to face Amy. "We're going to find out who's doing this, Ams."

"I know. But will it be before it's too late?" Worry lined her face.

His heart twisted at her quiet words. He wanted to protect her, to comfort her, to care for her. He prayed someday she'd forgive him, and he could be the man she deserved. Keith strode to her side and cupped her face. "Please don't think that way. I care for you too much to blow this. You have my word. I'll do everything I can to stop this maniac."

"But—"

"No, Ams. I made a huge mistake a year ago with Stacey. I put a rift between us. I'll never forgive myself for hurting you." He ran a hand over Carter's soft hair. "Carter's the only thing good about what happened." Keith met her gaze. "I'm sorry for causing you pain."

"I'm sorry, too." She sniffed, tears brimming on her lashes. "You're right, Carter is worth the pain, but what you and Stace did, it cut deep. I see the regret in your eyes. You didn't intend to hurt me, and I'm working on getting past it."

Keith exhaled. Her words weren't exactly what he wanted to hear, but he'd take the baby steps. However, he had to make her understand how much he cared for her. "I don't plan for Carter to lose another mother. And I don't plan to lose you." The idea turned his belly sour. He'd missed out on a relationship with Amy, and someday he hoped to turn that around. She had to live for him to prove he deserved her. And therein lay part of the problem. He had to convince himself of his worth.

"I know you will try your best." She nibbled on her lower lip. "But will it be enough?"

He dropped his hands and blew out a breath. Would his efforts be sufficient to keep her alive?

Leaving Amy in the living room, Keith made his way through the house, confirming the windows and doors were securely locked. Knowing Jason had the perimeter gave Keith a bit of peace, but the thought of Amy being killed twisted his heart.

God, I could really use some help. I can't lose her.

* * *

With Carter asleep in the living room, his grandpa and father watching over him, Amy slipped onto the covered back porch. Spotting Jason, she waved and leaned her head against the exterior of the house. Keith's words echoed in her brain. *I care for you too much for me to blow this.* Cared as a friend? Or something more? His eyes had spoken to the *more*, but had she misinterpreted his intent? Had she so desperately wanted him to want her—love her—that she'd imagined his interest?

Beyond that, could she let go of her pride and hurt, and let him into her heart? She stayed tucked out of sight and inhaled the fresh air. A nice change from being cooped up in the house. The birds chirped, and a squirrel jumped from limb to limb on a nearby tree. Amy smiled at the critter's antics. For one small moment, normal had seeped in, only to vanish in an instant. She missed her twin. And she longed for her photography career. The one she'd worked hard for and made a name for herself with. Her shoulders slumped. Having her life back seemed like a fantasy.

A hand landed on her shoulder.

Amy screamed and spun, fist raised.

"Chill, Ams. It's only me." Keith clasped both of her shoulders.

Sucking in oxygen, she caught her breath. "You scared me."

"Sorry about that, but what are you doing out here?"

"I needed to clear my head. Besides, I'm tucked in here out of sight."

"Ams." He cupped her cheek. "I get it. I really do. But you can't put yourself in danger." Keith motioned to the backyard with his opposite hand. "Even though you're staying at the back of the porch, you're still out in the open." He leaned in, his forehead almost touching hers. "We've been friends for years. I can't let anything happen to you."

"Friends." She huffed the word. Of course, she'd misinterpreted his intent earlier.

His eyes narrowed. "Don't look like that."

"Like what?"

"Like I stole your favorite teddy bear."

"I—"

Keith put his finger to her lips. "The answer to your question is yes, we're more than friends." Hope flickered in his gaze.

The warmth of his touch sent butterflies fluttering in her belly. Her heart pounded. Did she want more? She'd prayed for the day Keith would notice her, not as a childhood friend but as a woman he loved. She couldn't help herself. The question fell from her lips of its own accord.

"How much more?" She rested her hand on his forearm.

His muscle twitched beneath her touch, and his eyes darkened.

Keith lowered his head and waited. Silently asking her for permission to kiss her.

Amy hesitated. Did she want him to kiss her? Was she willing to put his and Stacey's actions aside? Who was she kidding? She rose on her tiptoes to close the gap.

"Get down!" Jason's yell startled her.

Keith threw her to the ground, and her head struck the wooden planks. White lights exploded behind her eyelids.

A crack echoed in the air.

Carter! Pinned to the ground, she struggled against Keith's weight. "Get off. I have to get to Carter." She forced the words out. Her head swam, and black dots pricked her vision.

"Hold on!" He slipped his weapon from his holster and moved off her.

Strong hands yanked her up and propelled her inside the house. She staggered across the room, praying for the world to stop spinning.

"Dad, watch her!" Keith's demand ratcheted up the pounding in her head.

"I've got her. Go." Ian steadied her. "Take it easy, honey. Carter's fine."

"Where, Jason?" The back door slammed shut, and Keith's voice faded.

She rushed into the living room, scooped up Carter and dropped onto the couch.

Emotions flooded her. Fear. Anger. Helplessness. All collided into one moment, leaving her reeling. She'd stepped out into the open and had almost gotten herself shot. And she'd put Keith in danger. *Stupid and selfish.* Amy pinched the bridge of her nose. When would it all end?

"Amy, darling?"

"I'm okay." Her voice cracked.

The older man pulled her close. Fatherly arms engulfed her, and she wilted against him. Oh, how she missed her family, but Keith's dad had claimed second parent's rights long ago. And right now, she craved a father's comfort. Sobs overtook her. Tears poured down her cheeks, soaking Ian's shirt.

"Let it out, my girl," Ian whispered in her ear, his words making her cry all the more.

The back door creaked open and clicked shut.

"Dad?" The worry in Keith's voice penetrated her brain, but the tears continued.

"She's okay, son. Just a bit overwhelmed if I had to guess."

Keith joined her on the couch. His strong arms encircled her and Carter.

She shifted and buried her face into his chest, Carter nestled between them.

"I'll go check on Jason." Ian's footsteps faded.

"Honey, please, you're scaring me. And worrying Carter." Keith's soft tone tugged at her heart.

"I—I'm sorry." She hiccuped another sob.

"You have nothing to be sorry for. I just want to know that you're not hurt."

She nodded and froze. The movement had set her head spinning again. "I hit my head, but other than that, I'm not injured."

"Let me see." He cupped her chin and tilted her head up. "You've got quite a goose egg on your forehead." He feathered his fingers across the lump. "Did I do that?"

"Yes, but thanks to Jason's warning and your quick reflexes, I'll live."

"Here." He handed her a handkerchief, compliments of his father, no doubt.

Amy mopped up her tears. "I'm a mess." She didn't need a mirror to know that her eyes were swollen and her face had red splotches. However, the crying jag had been cathartic.

"No, you're not. You're beautiful."

Had she heard him correctly?

With his hands on either side of her face, Keith's gaze turned serious. He closed the distance until they were nose to nose. "Don't ever do that again."

His proximity messed with her ability to think straight. "What?"

"Don't ever put yourself in danger like that again." His tone was demanding. "I can't lose you."

"Oh." She blinked.

Keith's lips covered hers. His kiss, far from gentle, made her insides turn to mush. The man she'd lost her heart to years ago was kissing her, and she was kissing him back.

A throat cleared, breaking the connection between her and Keith.

"What is it, Jason?" Keith stayed inches from her face.

"Couldn't find him. He's long gone for now."

"Thanks, man." Keith never broke eye contact with her.

"I'll call Sheriff Monroe and tell him what happened. Anyone need an ambulance?"

"No, I think we're good. If things change after the adrenaline fades, I'll let you know."

"Sounds like a plan. Doug will be here in an hour to take over. See you tomorrow. Carry on."

"Get out, partner," Keith grumbled.

"I'm a-gettin'." Jason chuckled and exited out the back door.

"I...uh..." Amy wanted to tell him he'd made her dream come true. Wanted to admit her feelings for him. But that would be a stupid move. She'd set herself up for heartbreak. How would she ever know that he wanted her and that she wasn't a replacement for her twin?

"Ams?" His pupils darkened.

"Yes?" She swallowed.

"The porch is off-limits. Stay where I know you'll be safe."

His words, those of a cop. His eyes...those of a friend? Or something more? Had she misjudged him? She had questions, things she wanted to ask, but she feared the answers. She closed her eyes and brushed her cheek on Carter's soft hair.

Keith kissed her temple and snuggled her and Carter against his chest. "Please don't do something that will get you killed."

And there it was again, like cold water thrown in her face.

Her attacker wanted her dead.

THIRTEEN

The morning chaos of breakfast and playing with Carter had disappeared. The current silence in the house grated on Keith's nerves. His father had insisted on taking a shift watching the perimeter, and Amy had taken Carter to the bedroom and planned to rock him to sleep for his morning nap. She'd been gone a good twenty minutes. Keith shook his head. Unbelievable. He already missed the little noises and even his son's cries to be fed. Who would have known he'd come to love the guy so quickly?

Oh, sure, he'd heard that parents fell in love with their children the moment they were born and even before, but he hadn't understood until he found out about Carter. His heart was fully involved. Not only for the little boy but the infant's aunt, too. They'd had moments where he thought she felt the same way, but every time she pulled away. All but once.

That kiss. He'd never forget her soft lips on

his. The connection that had sparked between them. He'd held her on the couch. The warmth of her against him comforted him and gave him hope. And when the moment passed, the door separating them slammed shut. One she refused to open. Keith rubbed his eyes and told his heart to let go of the feelings he had for Amy. Until she was ready, he had no hope of changing her mind. But why had she distanced herself from him?

The shooter situation had short-circuited his brain, and he'd kissed her without permission. She'd matched his intensity until he'd reminded her about the person after her. The moment had vanished. He'd failed her as a friend and as a detective. He blinked the grit from his eyes from the sleepless night. The shooting had his nerves on edge, and the kiss had turned his brain to goo.

A knock on the door had Keith ambling his way to the entry. He opened the door and found his friend and boss, Sheriff Monroe, on the other side.

"You look awful." Dennis eased past him with a file box in hand.

"Good morning to you, too." Keith latched the door closed. "Bringing gifts?"

"Thought you two needed a quiet day but also knew there was no way you'd sit back and let Jason take care of things."

He followed his boss to the kitchen. "You got that right. I trust my partner, but this is personal."

Dennis nodded and hefted the container onto the kitchen table. "Figured as much. I brought copies of all the reports and images from the multiple cases. Stacey Baker's, Trent Jefferies's and Debbie Ackers's. Plus, I added everything we've collected from the attacks on Amy."

Keith lifted the carafe. "Coffee?"

"Yes, please." Monroe eased onto a kitchen chair.

"Thanks for making the trip and the files." He filled two cups, replaced the carafe and handed a steaming mug to Dennis. The bold aroma wafted throughout the room. Keith tapped the side of his head. "We know the cases are linked up here. But we need solid proof. If we'd only catch a break on one of the murders, then we could find the creep and put an end to all this."

The sheriff took a sip and released a long breath. "We all want that for you and Amy."

"I know. You guys are great." Keith motioned to the upstairs. "It would have taken me forever to clean up that mess. And the extra hours patrolling...words can't express my gratitude." He rubbed his thumb along the rim of his mug. "We have a solid team, and I know we will put the person responsible behind bars..."

"But?"

"I feel like a failure for not doing it sooner."

Dennis chuckled.

"It's not funny, man. Amy's life depends on me—us—solving these cases." His grip around his cup tightened. He wanted to reach across the table and throttle his boss.

"At ease, Young. I'm taking the threats on Amy seriously. I find it amusing that the great Keith Young is head over heels in love with his childhood best friend."

"What?" Keith's voice rose. He glanced over his shoulder and softened his response. "I care for her. A lot. But love?"

Dennis's eyebrow arched.

Okay, so maybe his friend was right. Keith shook his head. Who was he kidding? He'd fallen in love with Amy years ago. And he'd thoroughly messed up his chances. "All right. So you might have a point."

"Might?"

"Okay. Okay, you're right. But I'm not sure it matters. She's still mad at me. Except for—"

"The kiss Jason walked in on?"

"He told you that?" Keith's partner had a big mouth. The next time he saw the man…

"You expected anything less? Jason wants the world to fall in love now that he has his dream girl."

"Yeah, he's determined to play matchmaker." Keith grinned. "He's like an old meddling biddy."

Dennis lifted his mug in salute. "True. He's

tried to set me up with four different women. The guy refuses to take no for an answer."

"No kidding. It's been three times for me. And that's in the last six months." Keith rolled his eyes.

"The man's happy." Dennis turned serious. "And what about you?"

Keith sighed. "To be honest, I'd like to join the club." He looked over his shoulder then back to his friend. "But I'm not sure she wants the same thing."

"Have you talked with her about it?"

"No. If you haven't noticed, there hasn't exactly been a great opportunity to have a conversation."

"But you've had time to kiss."

"There is that."

"Maybe you need to make time for that discussion."

"Hey, Sheriff." Amy stepped into the kitchen.

"No more formality, please."

"All right then—Dennis." She moved to the refrigerator and poured herself a glass of tea. "What do we owe the honor of your visit?"

"I brought y'all some light reading." Dennis gestured toward the box on the table. "And as much as I'd like to stay, I better get going, or Brenda will have the office rearranged by the time I get back." He tipped his mug and drained the remains of his coffee.

Amy tilted her head. "Brenda?"

"The office's new administrative assistant."

"Gotcha." Amy rested against the counter. "Guess Keith and I better get busy while little man's asleep."

Monroe's lip curved upward. "Or you can take a break and chat."

Keith pushed his chair back and snatched the empty cup. "Thanks for bringing the files by. I'll let you know if we find anything."

"You do that." Dennis pursed his lips, no doubt holding back a laugh. He slapped his thighs. "Welp, gotta go. You two kids be good."

If Dennis wasn't a friend, he'd throttle the man. The front door opened and closed. Keith placed the extra mug in the sink and refilled his own while gathering his thoughts.

"You okay?"

What could he say to that? *No. Someone's trying to kill you, and I love you but can't tell you.* Or could he? What did he have to lose? Her friendship—which was already on shaky ground after his world-class blunders.

"Let's have a seat." He gestured to the living room. Might as well go for it. "We need to talk."

Amy sunk onto the couch and swallowed hard against the desert that had inhabited her mouth. Keith's tone worried her. Had something happened on the case? Or did he regret the kiss she'd dreamed about all night? A kiss she'd longed for since—since always.

"Ams." Keith lowered himself beside her and shifted to face her. He grasped her hands in his. "I want to apologize—"

She narrowed her gaze at him. "Don't you dare apologize for that kiss."

"Not even a little." His lopsided smile eased her tension, at least a bit.

"Then what?"

He chuckled. "Well, if you'd let me finish."

"I—" Keith placed a finger to her lips. She huffed. That man was infuriating. Here she sat, twisted in knots, and he appeared calm like they shared kisses every day.

"Ams, slow down that brain of yours and listen. Give me a chance to explain before you rail me."

She snorted. "I don't do that."

His brows raised to his hairline.

"Okay, maybe a little now and then."

Keith bit his lip, hiding a smile.

She slugged his arm. "Stop that. You're impossible."

"Who me?" He feigned innocence.

The familiar banter wrapped Amy in a cocoon of warmth. Even though Keith had disappointed her and had broken her heart by choosing her twin, she didn't want to lose his friendship.

"So, what were you saying?" She held her breath, unsure of what she hoped for.

"I wanted to say I'm sorry for disappearing on you for the past year. I was ashamed of my actions with Stacey. I knew you'd see right through me and know what I'd done—what we had done. I had no intention of hurting you. I made a mistake and desperately want your forgiveness."

Amy longed for him to say that he'd always wanted her and not her twin. She wanted to hear those three little words, but her desire was no more than a dream. "Why is that so important to you?"

"Because I care about you."

Her shoulders slumped. She knew he cared. They'd been friends going on forever. "I care about you, too."

"I don't think you get it." Keith ran his fingers through her hair. "I really care about you."

A tingle of excitement and hope snaked up her spine. Did he mean what she hoped he meant? "Okay, I forgive you," she whispered, her lungs refusing to fill. The ticking clock and hum of the air conditioner blurred into the background. Her heartbeat the only audible thing in the room.

"Thank you." He leaned in, his lips centimeters from hers. Waiting for her to pull away. But she couldn't, not when she'd wanted more after sampling his tenderness last night.

The distance closed between them—she was unsure whether she'd moved forward, or he had. His arms wrapped around her and pulled her closer as he deepened the kiss.

A restrained passion lingered beneath his embrace. One she'd craved for the past eighteen years. First as a young girl and then as a woman. He'd never shown an interest, and expressing her own desire—out of the question. She refused to ruin a beautiful friendship over her ridiculous childhood crush. But now, it didn't seem so silly after all.

Keith pulled away and rested his forehead against hers. "I've wanted to do that for a long time."

Then why haven't you? The question sat on her lips, but she refused to ruin the moment.

He inhaled. "Shall we see what Dennis brought us?"

Amy's voice had escaped her, and all she could do was nod.

"Come on." He laced their fingers together, tugged her off the couch and led her to the kitchen.

They spent the day alternating reviewing the files and playing with Carter. The threat against her felt a world away, and the coziness too much like a family.

Did she dare hope for a future with Keith and Carter? Or would she get her heart broken all over again?

Too late. Amy's traitorous heart had already betrayed her. Keith was the only man for her.

For her entire life, she'd walked in Stacey's shadow. Now, if she could get past feeling like Keith's second choice, maybe they'd have a future together. But his kiss felt nothing like she was a consolation prize. It'd given her the sense that he cherished her and only her.

Her gaze traveled to the window, making her light mood dwindle. Unless they found a clue and arrested her attacker, she wouldn't have a future with Keith or anyone. She'd be dead.

FOURTEEN

With the printed pictures from Amy's cell phone in his hand, Keith strode into the kitchen and plopped down at the table. He added the photos to the stack of images they'd examined earlier.

Jason's words continued to niggle Keith's mind.

Tell her you love her. How could he when the fear of unworthiness had settled deep in his gut? He'd asked for forgiveness from God and Amy and had received it from both. Now, if only he could find it within to give himself mercy and put his poor choices in the past. See himself as deserving of a woman like Amy. Easier said than done.

Even if he put his uncertainty aside, Amy held a piece of herself back. She was a willing participant during their amazing kiss, but he sensed a slight hesitation. As if he'd placated her. Which was wrong on all fronts. Why had she thought such a thing?

Get out of your head, Young. Focus on the case.

Your love life, or lack thereof, is not important right now. He snorted. Tell his heart that. He shook his head and returned his attention to the documents Sheriff Monroe had delivered yesterday.

He and Amy had sorted the information and had studied it on and off throughout the day. Today, the same questions swirled in his head. Keith picked up a piece of paper, perused it and put it back.

One thing, God. Just a small clue that I can grasp hold of that will unravel these cases. Please.

Keith scratched the stubble on his jaw as he stared at the documents spread in front of him, searching for that one small thread to pull.

The files on the table taunted him. He had missed something—but what? He'd read through each piece multiple times. Keith flipped through the pictures that Amy had taken of the mayor's hunting wall, pausing on each one.

Even though they had all but crossed the mayor off the list, they had three suspects capable of killing. Mayor Nolan Taylor, his best friend and banker Christopher Dayton, and Taylor's son, Trevor. But Keith continued to miss the motive. Yes, they all had a reason, assuming Taylor had an affair with Debbie. Christopher protecting his friend from political humiliation. Trevor avoiding the embarrassment of his father's relationship with a woman only a few years older than Trevor himself. But were any of the reasons strong enough to kill? Only Nolan's. To avoid the disgrace of having an affair or keeping it from Sheila. Still, he hadn't found solid evidence of a scandal, only rumor. For Keith's conversation with the man, he agreed with Amy that it didn't feel like an affair had occurred.

Who had killed three times and planned to kill again? And why?

Was his focus too narrow? Should he expand his suspect base? But who else could it be? Kyle hadn't found anyone else outside the group who had motive. So that was a dead end, at least so far.

He ran his fingers through his hair and grabbed a handful. He'd pull out all his hair if it would help. The answers had to be there.

Stacey's picture stuck out beneath one of the reports. He scooted the papers aside and lifted his childhood friend's image. *I'm so sorry, Stacey. I should have been a better man that night. I wish you'd told me about Carter. I promise to love him enough for both of us.*

"You okay?" Amy's soft voice stopped his musing.

"Yeah. Just mad at myself." His gaze never left Stacey's picture. He couldn't face Amy and acknowledge his failure again—as a man and as a detective.

Her hands rested on his shoulders, and she

dropped a kiss to the top of his head. "What are you thinking?"

He reveled in her soft touch. The kind that a man could get used to. He wanted a replay of yesterday, but the case needed his attention.

"What's going on in that head of yours?" She smiled down at him.

Tossing Stace's image into the pile with the rest of the photographic evidence, he exhaled. "That I've barely kept you safe, and I can't figure out who killed the mother of my child."

Amy's hands dropped away.

Keith instantly missed the connection between them. He pivoted to face her. Tears filled her eyes. "What's wrong, Ams?"

"You loved her, didn't you?"

"Of course, you two were my best friends growing up." He scrunched his brows. He'd do anything for the two girls who crashed into his life as children and remained through adulthood. Amy wasn't making sense.

"That's not what I mean." Her jaw muscle clenched.

Apparently, he was no better at reading his best friend than he was at solving the case because he had no idea what Amy referred to. "I don't understand."

Amy fisted her hands, the expression on her

face one between anger and hurt. "Look, I'm sorry you lost her."

"I'm the one who's sorry. You lost your twin sister." He ached to comfort her, to hold her in his arms, the way he had yesterday, but her reaction confused him.

"And as you said, you lost the mother of your child." Amy hugged her waist. "I'm sorry the wrong twin died. It should have been me."

"Ams. How can you say that?" He reached for her, but she pulled away.

"Because it's true. Stace was the outgoing one. The one everyone gravitated to. The brave one." Tears streamed down Amy's cheeks.

"Ams, please. You are an incredible woman. You're talented, caring and you love adventure. No, you aren't the daredevil Stace was, but who cares?"

"I've always lived in her shadow. And even now, you'd rather have her." Amy's voice ratcheted up.

"Are you serious?" How had Keith let it get this far without telling Amy the truth? "Amy, I thought we had something between us. That kiss had to mean something."

"It meant that I'm a fool. I'm not going to be the woman that you look at and wish for my twin. I refuse to be your second choice."

Second choice? It had never been Stacey that he'd wanted. It had always been Amy. If he said his night with Stacey hadn't meant anything to him, he'd come across as a class A jerk. But if he told Amy she had always been his choice, she wouldn't believe him because of his night with Stace. Stuck. That's what he was.

Frustrated and irritated, Keith shoved his chair from the table. Growing up, he'd never had issues telling the twins what was on his mind. He'd just blurt out what he thought. Now—not so much. He guessed that's what happened when you messed things up with your best friends. He'd better get out of there and figure out what to say before he made things worse. He grabbed his weapon and slid it into the holster attached to his belt. "I'm going to help Jason check the perimeter."

He spun from Amy's wide eyes and headed for the back door. Keith had to leave before he said something that pushed Amy further away.

Stomping outside, he searched out Jason. The sun pressed down on Keith as he spotted his partner at the far edge of the property.

Keith marched across the yard, his boots crunching on the grass. He stood, hands on his hips under an oak tree near the far fence. "I'm relieving you from patrol." He grumbled, hoping his partner would take the hint and head out.

"What's got you all bent out of shape?" Jason crossed his arms over his chest.

He should have known it wouldn't be that easy. "Amy."

"Well, I figured that."

Birds chirped in the tree above, and a daring squirrel jumped from the roof of the shed to a limb. Tail twitching, the critter bobbed up and down on the branch before springing to the next one. Keith closed his eyes and released a long breath. "She thinks she's my second choice in twins."

"Is she?"

He jerked his gaze to Jason. "No. She's the one I've always wanted. Stacey was a drunken mistake. Amy's the one that I'm attracted to. The only one I've ever wanted a future with."

"Have you told her that? Not the drunken mistake part with her sister, but the other." Jason glared at him.

"Yes." He thought he'd made it perfectly clear. What else could he have meant by that kiss?

"Really?"

Keith shrugged. "Maybe not in so many words."

Jason smacked his forehead. "Dude, you need to tell her exactly what you're thinking." He held up a hand to stop Keith's comment. "Women like to be told."

"And you're the expert now?" Keith rolled his eyes.

"No. Let's just say that Mel has taught me a lot. I'm not the perfect husband, that's for sure.

And she'd gladly agree to that observation. One thing I've learned is that for Melanie, actions speak to her head, but the words fill her heart."

"You sound like a sap." When had his partner turned into a TED Talk?

"Listen, call it what you want, but I plan to love my wife the way she deserves."

Keith sighed. "Yeah, yeah. You've got a point."

"How long have you known Amy?"

"Over twenty years."

"Long enough to know what she needs and what she wants," Jason challenged.

He and the twins had gone through childhood and their teen years together. They'd complained about dating during high school and discussed colleges and their futures with each other. He knew both Amy and Stacey better than anyone. "You might have a point."

"Of course I do." His partner smirked and slapped him on the back. "I'll stay for a little while. Have a feeling your focus will be lacking. Call if you need anything."

Keith nodded and watched his friend round the side of the house.

Jason was right. Keith had blown it again with his insecurity of telling Amy exactly how he felt. She'd forgiven him, but the real problem was he hadn't forgiven himself.

Time to have a heart-to-heart with God and

get his head on straight. Then he'd go in and say what he'd longed to tell her for years.

Until then, he had a job to do. Protecting Amy and his son topped his priority list.

To think Amy had pondered the meaning of Keith's kiss and their time together all night. She'd even thought he wanted her. Not as a substitute for her twin, but her. Amy's heart had soared at the idea that her dreams might come true. But when she'd walked in on him this morning, her heart had shattered when he'd chastised himself about not being able to save the mother of his child. To think, the whole time, his heart had wanted Stacey. Had he envisioned kissing Stacey when he held Amy last night?

Amy had never been jealous of her twin. Well, not exactly. There were times she'd craved her sister's extroverted nature, but overall, she'd been happy with herself the way God had made her. Until Amy found out about Carter's father. She sighed. The one thing Amy had dreamed about— a future with Keith—had been ripped from her. So, yes, she was jealous of Stacey for the first time in her life.

But Stacey died because of Amy.

Guilt slammed into her. She picked up her twin's picture. Stacey's sheet-covered lower body hid the brutal fact the killer had attempted to burn the evidence, including Amy's sister. Bile rose in her throat. How could Amy think of herself right now? Stacey, a piece of her, was gone, forever.

Tears pricked her eyes. The killer's mistake had decimated all that remained of her family—except Carter. Amy had lost her sister and gained a son all in that moment. All because Amy had witnessed a murder. She traced her finger down the picture of Stacey.

I'm so sorry for only thinking of myself, Stace. I promise to figure out who did this so Keith can put the person responsible behind bars.

Putting down the picture, Amy picked up the report and read. Ten minutes later, she exchanged one file for another. Debbie Ackers, then Detective Trent Jefferies. She mixed the three tragic deaths with her own recall of what had happened. She placed her hands wide on the edge of the table and let her gaze roam from one pile to the next. The facts stared back at her. No clue jumped out. Not even a hint to point to the person responsible. Amy pinched the bridge of her nose. Her life, a ticking time bomb, with the timer approaching zero.

I want my life back. Correction, I want to live, and my sister deserves justice. What are we missing, God?

Something niggled at the back of her mind

just beyond her grasp. She sat up straight in her chair and rearranged the documents on the table into stacks of evidence, suspects, Stacey's file, Trent's file and Debbie's file, then she grabbed a notepad. She jotted down her thoughts on suspects and motives. One by one, she crossed out her different ideas, leaving her with zilch.

Amy tapped her pen on her chin. Now what? She tried a different angle. Deciding on a free-flow brainstorm, she scribbled down any words and phrases that came to mind. Stacey. Camera. Two people. Connection to Eagle Bay. Cliff. Trail. Detective. Police Department. Mayor. Shotgun. Arrow. Old truck. Handgun. Knows the area. Knew Debbie. Hunter. Pictures.

She circled the words *hunter* and *pictures*. Did the images from the mayor's office hold the answer? She grabbed the photos Keith had printed from her phone.

The image was similar to the one in Sheriff Monroe's office. Debbie's smiling face beamed back at her as the woman stood next to Mayor Taylor. Odd Nolan had chosen that picture and not a family one to grace his desk. Her gaze shifted between Nolan and Debbie, and she circled their faces with the wax pencil. What was it about this picture that had caught her attention?

Next, she examined the pictures she'd snapped from the mayor's wall. Mayor Taylor, Trevor and

Christopher, front and center, decked out in their hunting gear, smiled at her. Their hunting prowess was legendary. If she believed the town scuttle-butt, any one of them could kill with accuracy. But which one? And why? She couldn't wrap her head around the mayor killing Debbie even if the man held a secret. Trevor? His father having an affair might give him motive, but that still didn't add up. And then there was Christopher. Other than pro-tecting his friend, what possible reason would he have for murder? Money? Love? No, that didn't seem right either. Amy took another look, this time focusing on the background of each snap-shot. Wax pencil in hand, she circled each person.

A gasp escaped her lips. The truth slammed into her. How had they missed it? They'd had it all wrong this whole time, assuming her hunch was correct.

Amy's gaze drifted to the window and she spotted Jason heading to his car. She peeked into the living room. Ian sat on the floor playing with his grandson. With Carter safe under his grand-father's watchful eye, she hurried out the back and slipped into the passenger seat of Jason's car.

"May I help you?" Jason rested his wrist on the top of the steering wheel and twisted to look in her direction.

"Let's go see the mayor." She prayed he'd drive and not ask questions.

His eyebrow arched. "What about Keith?"

Amy sighed. "I don't want to deal with him right now, okay?"

"You love him, don't you?"

"No. Yes. It's complicated. Besides, it doesn't matter."

"Why on earth not?"

"He's still in love with my twin."

Jason made a sound between a duck and a strangled cat. "He told you that?"

"No. He... Never mind. Just drive."

"Oookay." Jason cranked the engine and pulled out of the driveway. "Are you at least going to let him know you left?"

She crossed her arms over her chest and glared at him.

"Tell ya what, I'll call him and give him the heads-up."

Keith's farmhouse faded in the distance.

"You do that." She couldn't talk to Keith. Not yet.

Jason tapped his phone and connected to his Bluetooth.

An old green pickup came out of nowhere.

"Jason!"

"Hold on!" He yanked the wheel.

The truck T-boned the rear driver's-side door with a sickening crunch of metal.

She screamed.

The car spun and skidded off the road. A final jolt jerked her forward, then back against the seat, sending a ripple of pain where the seat belt snapped across her chest.

"Jason?" Amy strained to see what had happened to him. She gasped.

He slumped motionless over the steering wheel. Glass glittered in his hair and over the seat and dashboard. Blood trickled from the gash on his forehead.

She had to get help. Amy patted her left front jeans pocket for her phone. Her fingers tapped the device. She blew out a long breath. *Yes!*

The passenger door squeaked open. "Get out!"

Amy jumped and jerked her attention to the voice.

Sheila jabbed the weapon into Amy's temple. "Don't do anything stupid, or I'll shoot you where you sit." The woman jutted her chin toward Jason. "And he's next."

Amy scanned the area, praying for help. With no one in sight, her hopes shattered. She unbuckled herself and hefted her aching body from the car.

The mayor's wife shoved her toward the green pickup truck.

She stumbled but righted herself before hitting the ground. How did Sheila plan to get away? The woman's truck couldn't be drivable. Amy examined the vehicle. The grille guard had taken the impact and appeared unscathed.

"Get in. You're driving."

Why had she allowed her insecurities to dictate her actions? If she'd told Keith her suspicions, she wouldn't be in this mess. And Jason wouldn't be hurt.

Amy climbed in behind the wheel. Tears pricked her eyes. If Sheila succeeded, Amy would never see Carter again. *I'm sorry, Stacey.* At least the little guy had his father. Her heart dropped to her feet. So much for Keith coming to the rescue. He had no idea she had left with Jason.

With the gun in her side, Amy wove through town, following Sheila's directions to drive to the trailhead where the whole thing had begun.

She'd die like Debbie, and no one would know that Sheila was behind it all.

All Amy could do was pray that Jason was okay and able to get word to Keith.

I need some help here, Lord.

Her phone. If she could get to it without drawing Sheila's attention, she might have a chance.

FIFTEEN

The screen door slammed shut behind Keith. He'd stomped around the yard for the past hour, getting his emotions under control. He'd had a long talk with God and had made the decision. He owed Amy the truth. Once he arrested the person responsible for the attacks, he and Amy needed to have a long serious conversation, but for now, she deserved to know how he felt. They could work out the details later, assuming she believed him.

Keith paused at the kitchen table, taking note of the neat stacks. He inspected them a little closer. Someone had arranged them in a different order. The notepad with Amy's handwriting jumped out at him. He twisted it toward him to see what she had written. The woman had put a few pieces together, and it appeared she was onto something. Interesting. He had to hear her thoughts on what she'd discovered. But first, he had to find her and admit his feelings.

The hum of the air conditioner broke the silence in the house. No happy squeals or cries from his son. No chatter of Amy and his dad. Where had everyone gone? His footfalls echoed on the floor in the unusual quiet, creating an eerie sensation like something out of a suspense movie.

"Ams?" When she didn't answer, Keith peeked into the living room. His father napped in the recliner with Carter in his arms.

He headed upstairs and softly knocked on his bedroom door, where Amy and Carter now stayed. No answer. He turned the knob and peered inside. "Ams?" Keith furrowed his brow. His farmhouse was on the larger side, but not so big someone could disappear. Worry twisted his gut. What if the attacker found a way in and took her? His pulse ratcheted up a notch. He hurried downstairs.

"Dad?" Keith jiggled the man's arm.

Ian blinked. "Yes."

"Have you seen Amy?"

His father rubbed the sleep from his eyes. "No. Sorry, son."

Keith's phone rang. He glanced at the caller ID. "Hey, Jason. Have you seen Amy?"

"She's gone."

"What are you talking about?"

"We were heading into town to talk to the

mayor when a green truck rammed us. I just woke up. She's missing."

"She's what?" Keith's blood pressure rose.

"Dude. Stop yelling. My head's pounding."

His friend was hurt, and Amy had disappeared. Keith's day had gone from bad to worse. "Where are you? Do you need an ambulance?"

"About a mile from your place. And no, I'm good. I think."

"Stay put. I'm coming to get you." Keith disconnected.

"What's wrong?" Ian came and stood next to him.

"Jason's hurt, and Amy's missing." He relayed the small amount of information to his father.

Keith clenched his hands into a fist. "Of all the stupid—"

"I'm not sure she's the only one to blame for not telling you." His father pointed a steely glare at him.

Yeah, he hadn't handled the situation well. Guilt and shame had reared their ugly heads, and he hadn't owned up to his true feelings. If only he'd been honest from the start. He threw up his hands. "No. Probably not. Listen, I've got to go find her before her attacker finishes the job."

Ian rubbed Carter's back, soothing him back to sleep after Keith's raised voice had stirred him from his baby slumber. "Be careful. I'll be praying."

"Thanks, Dad." Keith sprinted from the house. He jumped into his truck and flew down the drive, kicking up dust in his wake. He'd really messed things up. His best friend, with whom he'd shared dreams and hurts throughout their childhood and teen years, hadn't been willing to come talk to him. She'd gone to Jason instead.

The sight of Jason's wrecked car twisted his gut. Keith slammed the truck into Park and rushed to the vehicle.

"Cooper?"

"Yeah, I'm here. Kinda stuck, though." Jason's slowed speech worried Keith.

He needed the crowbar from his truck. "Hold on."

"I'm not going anywhere."

A few minutes later, he had the driver's-side door pried open and Jason out of the car.

"What can you tell me?"

"Not much." Jason gingerly touched the cut on his head. "One minute we're driving along, and the next we are spinning into the ditch. Next thing I know, Amy is gone."

Keith had to find her. "Come on. Let's get you to the house and cleaned up. We need to go over the files and her notes."

After getting Jason patched up, Keith sat at the kitchen table studying the notes and stacks of evidence and files. What had she figured out?

He lifted Amy's notes and committed her scribbles to memory.

Jason lowered himself onto a chair. "I don't like this."

"Neither do I. Where is she?" Keith rubbed a hand across the back of his neck. "Why did she leave without me?"

Jason seemed to realize Keith had asked the question more to himself and didn't answer. "You said she had figured something out. You know what it was? Why she wanted to see Mayor Taylor?"

"No." The photos Amy had taken in the mayor's office grabbed his attention. "But she has the word *pictures* written on the notepad." He laid the images side by side. "What did you see, Ams?" Keith studied each photo, praying the answer would jump out at him.

His partner joined him. "All I see are a group of men who like to hunt." Jason turned to face him. "What else does she have on that paper?"

"She wrote down *Shotgun. Arrow. Handgun. Hunter. Pictures.* Those are the ones that stand out."

Jason narrowed his gaze at the images and pulled out his phone. "I'm calling Kyle. See if he has any more background info on Debbie or the mayor's family and friends yet."

"I'll call the mayor." Keith placed the call to the mayor's office. "Mayor Taylor, this is Detective Young."

"Good to hear from you. What can I do for you, Detective?"

"I need your help. Can you tell me where your son and Christopher are?"

"Well, Trevor is easy. He's sitting across from me."

"Could you put the phone on speaker, please?"

"I'm not sure what you're fishing at, but okay." Keith heard the click.

"All right. You have us both."

"What's all this about?" Trevor's irritation rang over the line.

"Let's just say I'm eliminating you both as suspects."

"I've told you before, we had nothing to do with Debbie's death."

"I understand, sir, but I wouldn't be doing my job if I didn't ask the questions."

The mayor gave a loud sigh. "True. What else do you want to know?"

"Who else have you taken to your cabin?"

"Besides our family, Christopher. The location is our private escape. We don't invite others."

"And Christopher is where?"

"The bank, I assume, and before you ask, I have no idea where Sheila is. I suggest you try the nail salon or the house."

"I will. Thank you, Mayor."

"I'd say anytime, but I'd be lying."

"I understand." Keith hung up at the same time Jason said goodbye to Kyle. "Well?"

"Kyle didn't find any old boyfriends or enemies for Debbie. The only interesting thing he dug up was a long-lost cousin of Sheila's in Eagle Bay. He's going to investigate that thread more."

"That doesn't sound like a coincidence. You don't think Sheila's involved, do you?"

The question hung in the air.

Jason rubbed his jaw. "I'd say no, but—"

Keith's phone buzzed. He glanced at the screen. "It's Amy." He punched the button. "Ams, where are you?"

"Don't do this, Sheila. Think of Nolan." Amy's muffled voice carried over the line.

"As if he ever thought about me. All he cared about was that tramp daughter of his." Anger spewed with Sheila's words.

The hair prickled on the back of Keith's neck. He muted the phone. "Sheila *is* the killer. She has Amy." He switched the phone to speaker and turned up the volume but kept it on mute.

Jason's eyes widened. "Are you kidding me? Prim, proper Sheila?" His partner whipped out his phone. "Annie, get a BOLO out on Sheila Taylor. She's the one responsible for the attacks on Amy and possibly more." A short pause and Jason responded, "Got it. I'll keep you posted."

Keith clutched the phone tight enough he

thought it might splinter into pieces in his hand. He wanted to move, to rush out and rescue her from danger, but he had no idea where to start looking. "Come on, Ams, give us a clue." A hand landed on his shoulder and gave a supportive squeeze. He glanced at his partner and nodded his thanks. He appreciated Jason's steadiness. Especially since Keith was seconds from falling apart.

"You're going to kill me on the cliff like you did Debbie."

Keith turned to Jason. "The cliff. We've got to stop Sheila." Keith's lungs refused to fill, causing his words to come out as a whisper. Amy's words drove a dagger into his heart. How had they missed it? As a detective, he knew better than to only look at the obvious. He'd failed Amy again.

"Go. I'm right behind you."

Keith took off out the door with Jason keeping pace right behind him, the phone still on speaker.

"Fitting, isn't it. You should have died that day," Sheila said.

"But you killed the wrong twin." Keith heard Amy choke back a sob.

"Unfortunate, but yes."

"And what about Trent Jefferies? You killed him, too?"

"He was getting too close to the truth, asking too many questions. I had to eliminate him. With a little inside help it was easy to get him to come to the hotel. You should have seen the fear in his eyes right before he died." Sheila chuckled. "What a loser. Now, enough talking." A car door creaked. "Get out and march up that trail." Two doors slammed shut. Rustling filled the airwaves.

Keith's heart threatened to beat out of his chest. He had to save Amy. He had to save the woman he loved. He'd loved her since they were kids, and he planned to tell her if—not if, when— he brought her back home safe and sound. He'd make her understand that he'd only ever wanted her.

He and Jason arrived at the truck. "I'm driving," Jason said.

He slid into the passenger seat. His partner gunned the engine and sped through town, lights flashing. Keith willed the vehicle to go faster. He had to prevent Sheila from killing the woman he wanted a future with.

Please, God, don't take Amy from me. Give me the chance to tell her I love her and show her I can be the man she deserves.

SIXTEEN

Amy prayed she'd hit the right button on her cell phone in her pocket, and Keith was listening.

Limbs reached out like fingers over the path. Under normal circumstances, the foliage felt relaxing, but today the trees closed in, threatening to squeeze the life out of her. Air sucked from her lungs. And her heart was in jeopardy of beating out of her chest.

The barrel of the gun dug into Amy's back. She winced. She had to stall the trek up the trail. Give Keith a chance to get there. Assuming the call had connected. Tears burned behind her eyes. If she died today, she knew God waited for her on the other side of life, but she didn't want to leave Carter. Didn't want to leave Keith. Her stomach churned. She wanted to throw up. How had she been so stupid to let her insecurities get in the way of telling him how much she loved him? Had always loved him. Did it matter if she was his second choice? She'd have her dream if she let go of her lack of self-esteem. However, it wouldn't matter if Sheila succeeded.

"You don't have to do this, Sheila." Amy swiped at the tear that snuck out and trickled down her cheek.

"Shut up!" Evil simmered beneath the command.

Come on, Amy. Think. If she wanted to tell Keith she loved him, she had to give him time to save her from her own stupidity. She'd put herself in danger because of hurt and unwillingness to be honest with him.

An idea popped into her head. Not that the idea gave her much of a delay, but anything helped. She slowed her pace little by little, hoping Sheila hadn't noticed.

"Stop dawdling. Get moving." Sheila shoved her.

Amy stumbled and fell. The loose gravel cut into her knees and palms. Not exactly how she'd planned it, but whatever worked. She'd take the sting in her hands if it created time. Swallowing the lump in her throat, she pushed up onto all fours.

Sheila clocked Amy in the side of the head. "That's for messing around." The woman grabbed her arm and yanked her to her feet. Amy stumbled off the trail and into the vegetation along the edge. The world spun, and darkness descended.

"Wake up!" A boot jabbed her ribs.

How long had she lost consciousness? She blinked away the cobwebs inhabiting her brain. No way to tell.

"Get up!"

Amy pushed up on all fours, then placed her hand on a nearby tree and rose to her feet. She fought the nausea swirling in her belly. The earthy scent of the soil intensified around her. Her head throbbed in time with her heartbeat. She'd miscalculated the severity of Sheila's response. But maybe it had been long enough for Keith to find her. Maybe not.

"Quit stalling." The mayor's wife clutched Amy's forearm, jabbed the gun into her side then pushed her forward.

The trail whirled in front of her. Each step like walking through a vortex tunnel at an amusement park. Amy struggled to stay upright. But she had no choice. The woman would kill her before Keith arrived if she failed to keep moving. Assuming he arrived. Amy shook the negative thought away and instantly regretted it. She swallowed the bile rising in her throat.

She focused on putting one foot in front of the other as she trudged up the hill. She had no brainpower to think beyond the task in front of her. She made it around the curve, and the wooded path opened up into a green meadow with dots of pink, purple and yellow.

If her life ended here, at least beauty surrounded her. The swirling dream overwhelmed her. Her body begged to lie down, and her eyes pleaded with her to allow them to close. *What will it be like to meet God face-to-face?* Amy jerked at the direction her mind had wandered and blinked away the daze. She wanted to smack herself for the helpless thought that popped into her mind. When had she given up? *Sorry, God. I can't wait to meet You, but I'd prefer if it wasn't today.*

No doubt she had a mild concussion, considering the hallucinations she fought. The world continued to blur, and she wanted to give in, but she had to stay in the present and look for an opportunity to get away.

Sheila pushed Amy toward the cliff, eliminating time and opportunity to escape. Had this been what it was like for poor Debbie? Aware her life would end, and no one would know? At least Amy had Keith looking for her.

An array of floral scents rose in the air from the wildflowers that layered the field. Amy's footfalls smashed sections of grass, leaving a path from the trail. She glanced toward the trees and brush area along the perimeter of the meadow. *Come on, Keith. Save my bacon.* Movement to her right caught her attention. She blinked away the haze still threatening to take her under and narrowed her gaze.

A bird took flight, and Amy's hope nose-dived. She was by herself with the woman who wanted her dead.

Sweat beaded on her forehead. Where was Keith? Had he received her call, or was she going to die out here, all alone?

Keith's heart had quit beating when Amy had cried out and gone silent. A steady stream of Sheila's cursing had filled the air.

Whatever Amy had done, her antics had given Keith and Jason the time they needed to get to the cliff.

The bird had almost given away Keith's position behind the bush ten feet from where Sheila held Amy at gunpoint.

Phone on silent, he texted Jason, who had taken up watch among the trees across the meadow from Keith. I have eyes on her.

An instant response came from Jason. Same. I'm moving closer to the cliff.

Copy that.

Knowing his partner had his back, Keith crouched and snuck along the edge, staying out of sight. He racked his brain for a way to signal Amy. He hated the thought of her feeling abandoned. But anything he did would put her at further risk.

Hold on, Ams.

Stealthily as possible, Keith darted to the boulder by the edge of the cliff. Thankful for the tree line that hid his progress, he sat and leaned his back against the large rock. As a deputy, stressful situations weren't new to him. But having the woman he loved held at gunpoint? His mind spun with horrible endings to the scene on the other side of the boulder, and his pulse rate was fast enough to win the Indy 500. He closed his eyes and forced his heart to slow and his mind to quit conjuring up worst-case scenarios. Amy had helped them find her. Now it was on him to save her from a devious and dangerous woman.

"Sheila, listen to me. You won't get away with this." The quiver in Amy's voice almost made Keith rush in, but his training kicked in, and he reined in his emotions.

One long deep breath, and he put on his detective persona. Calm. Cool. All business. His focus pivoted from fear to a solution.

"No one knows it's me." Sheila's tone turned cocky.

"That's where you're wrong. They've heard everything you've said." He imagined Amy's chin raised in defiance.

"What!" Sheila's voice skyrocketed. Birds scattered from the trees, filling the air with squawking and the fluttering of their wings.

"My phone in my pocket. I called Keith. He knows it's you. He's been listening the whole time." Her voice wavered, losing the bravado it had seconds ago.

Yes, Ams, I heard you. I'm here. Keith peeked around the rock and eyed the situation. A plan took form, but he had to get closer.

He dug out his phone and texted Jason. I need a distraction.

Thirty seconds.

Copy that.

The weight of his SIG Sauer in his hand gave him the confidence he needed to get Amy out of the situation alive. Alive so he could tell her he loved her. No more holding back. And if she rejected him, so be it. It would kill him inside, but he'd learn to live with it. Staying silent was no longer an option for him.

Keith closed his eyes. Twenty seconds. He pulled in a deep breath. Fifteen. He crouched into position. Ten seconds.

"You brat!" Sheila grabbed a handful of Amy's hair and jabbed the gun against her temple.

Amy cried out.

His heart ripped in two at the pain-filled

scream, but he shoved the feeling away. Five, four, three, two, one.

A tree limb flew through the air and landed with a thud.

Thank you, Jason.

Sheila's attention flew to the sound.

Keith burst from behind the boulder and raised his gun. "Police! Put down the weapon, Sheila!"

Sheila responded faster than he'd expected. She wrapped her arm around Amy's throat and pushed the muzzle harder into the side of her head. "Don't come any closer!"

"It's over, Sheila. You aren't walking away from this a free woman." Keith inched closer. His gaze darted to Jason. His partner didn't have a clean shot, and neither did he.

Amy struggled to breathe and clawed at her attacker's arms.

Sheila's hold tightened, strangling the life from Amy.

His best friend stared at him wide-eyed, gasping like a fish on the bank.

A band constricted around his chest, forcing the air out of his lungs. He had to quit looking at the woman he loved and focus on the threat. The world silenced around him, his attention solely on the scene before him. He softened his tone. "Put the gun down and let Amy go. I know you don't want to hurt her."

Sheila threw her head back, and a bizarre high-pitched cackle emanated from her.

The inhuman sound sent shivers up his spine. His experience told him there would be no talking the woman down. He had to get Amy away from the unhinged woman.

Keith leaped toward Sheila and grabbed her gun hand. "Run, Ams!"

Amy fought against Sheila's python grip. Prying at her attacker's arm.

He tried to help, but Sheila's strength surprised him, and he had to maintain his focus on the weapon she possessed.

With a Herculean determination, Amy wrenched herself from Sheila's hold and stumbled away.

Keith continued his struggle with Sheila. With Amy out of the way, he had more options to take the woman down.

The gun went off and a bullet whizzed past him. "Enough!" He twisted Sheila's arm behind her. Jason rushed over and zip-tied her wrists together.

"Took you long enough." Keith holstered his SIG, panting from the exertion.

Jason glared at him. "I'm here, aren't I? And we have her in custody."

The sudden realization that Amy hadn't joined him had him spinning to find her. "Amy?" He spotted her lying on the ground. Crimson liquid soaked her shirt. He hurried to her side. "Jason, call an ambulance! Wake up, Ams. Talk to me." He lifted the hem of her shirt and sucked in a breath. A huge gash oozed with blood. He laid his hand on her side and put pressure on her wound. "Hang on, honey."

Deputies rounded the corner of the trail and sprinted toward them.

Jason handed off Sheila to the officers and knelt next to him. "How is she?"

"I don't know." Keith's hands shook against her skin. "She's bleeding and hasn't responded."

His partner unclipped his phone from his belt and dialed dispatch. "Where's that ambulance?" His head turned. "Got it." He pointed toward the trail. "Here they come."

Brent and Ethan rushed toward them.

"Talk to me." Ethan dropped his duffel and joined Keith at Amy's side.

"Gunshot wound to her left side. And from the looks of the gash on her head, she took a hit to her temple. Who knows what else."

"Got it. We'll take it from here." Ethan whipped out gauze and swapped places with Keith.

He scooted back and allowed the paramedics to attend to Amy. Keith held out his blood-covered palms. His hands trembled as the reality of what had happened took hold.

Jason stood next to him and rested his hand on Keith's shoulder. "She's gonna be okay."

"I hope so." Eyes never leaving the woman he wanted to call his wife and have children with, he wiped his hands on his thighs, transferring the red sticky substance to his pants, and prayed he'd get the opportunity to tell her he loved her.

When Deputy Lewis arrived to maintain the crime scene's integrity, Keith and Jason followed the medics down the trail in silence and watched them load the gurney.

"Go on. I'll meet you at the hospital." Jason nudged him toward the open doors of the ambulance.

Unable to speak, Keith hopped in and lowered himself onto the bench seat. His partner closed the door. He placed Amy's hand in his and squeezed. Sirens whined as the medic unit raced toward the hospital with the woman he loved, unconscious and bleeding.

He bowed his head and closed his eyes. *God, my shame and guilt got in the way, and Amy's lack of trust in me put her in danger. Don't let her die because of my unwillingness to tell her the truth.*

SEVENTEEN

A hot poker burned in Amy's side, and the little men inside her head pounded on her temples with tiny hammers. She swallowed past the burn in her throat. What had happened? The last thing she remembered was Keith walking out on her. The memory of his final words about Stacey rattled in her brain. The ache in her heart joined the pain in her abdomen and head.

"Why isn't she awake?" The familiar timbre of her childhood friend filtered through the haze.

"Unsure. She has a contusion on her temple, bruises on her neck and the gunshot wound in her side."

"How bad is the gunshot wound?"

I've been shot?

"It doesn't appear to have penetrated, but it's a deep gouge. Lots of blood, but not life-threatening." A deep voice that sounded familiar, but Amy couldn't place it.

"Thank You, God."

Wait. Keith. He was here. He hadn't left her.

Amy struggled against the cement sealing her lids closed. She inhaled. The fire in her side ignited, and she whimpered.

A hand warmed her arm. "Take it easy, Ams. You're okay." Keith's worried tone melted her heart.

She swallowed, and her throat screamed at her. She forced her eyes to cooperate and found herself gazing into Keith's concerned blue-gray eyes.

He brushed the hair from her forehead. "There you are. You had me worried."

"It hurts," Amy whispered.

"I know, honey. We'll get you to the hospital and fixed up soon." He brought her hand to his lips and kissed her fingers. "Don't try to talk." She watched as Keith lifted his gaze and talked to the person on the other side of her. "Can you give her something for the pain?"

A few seconds later, a cool sensation crawled up her arm, and the world became warm and fuzzy. The discomfort lessened, and she faded toward the cloud of bliss.

"That's it, sweetheart, relax. Go ahead. Go back to sleep."

What if he left? She had to talk to him. "Keith?"

He placed a kiss on her forehead. "I'm not going anywhere. 'Cause once you are feeling better, I need to tell you something."

Her mind tumbled further down the hole of

nothingness. She tried to grasp his words but failed. She latched on to his commitment to stay with her. Contentment flooded her. Giving up, she allowed the darkness of sleep to take her under.

Amy blinked. The room came into focus. She rolled her head to the side and regretted the movement. The world spun. She stilled and took a deep breath. After regaining her equilibrium, she tried again.

A hospital room took shape, and she took inventory of her injuries. Her head pounded, her side ached and her throat was sore. Everything hurt, but the pain had dulled. Thanks to the meds, no doubt.

A nurse entered the room. Her name tag said Janie. "How are you feeling?"

Amy wondered if it was the same lady who took care of her when she'd wrecked her car. "Like I've been dragged behind a truck," she whispered. Sheila's attempt to strangle her had left her unable to speak in normal tones.

"Don't force yourself to talk. Give it time to heal." Janie helped raise the head of the bed, then filled a cup and held the straw to Amy's lips.

She leaned forward a smidge and took a sip. The cool liquid coated her raw throat. "Thank you." She rested against the pillow. The small movements wore her out. "Where's Keith?"

"Detective Young?" The woman adjusted Amy's IV.

"Yes."

"He left a little while ago." Janie finished her tasks and patted her leg. "Let me know if you need anything." She smiled and exited the room.

Amy's heart dropped. Keith had said he wouldn't leave her. Hadn't he? Tears burned behind her eyes. Had he abandoned her—again? A sob erupted. She loved him and planned to tell him, but she'd lost her opportunity. He was gone.

Keith regretted leaving Amy, but he knew Carter would lift her spirits. He hoped to return before she woke. He'd only planned to be gone for twenty minutes—grab his son and rush back. He had so many things to tell her that he was bursting to let it out.

Twenty minutes had turned into forty.

He scooped Carter from the car seat and grabbed the diaper bag. "Come on, buddy, let's go see your momma."

The little guy snuggled into the crook of Keith's neck. His heart melted even more than he'd thought possible. Keith carried his son into the hospital and headed up to Amy's room. The elevator door opened, and he entered the waiting room on the third floor.

Paper coffee cup in hand, Jason leaned against the wall, ankles crossed. "'Bout time you got back."

Worry rippled up Keith's spine. Were Amy's

injuries more severe than Doc Jefferson had first stated? "Why? What's wrong?"

"I went to check on Amy while you were gone."

"And?" Keith jiggled Carter, more for his own nerves than to calm his son. Jason was supposed to watch over her until he got back.

Jason chucked his cup in the trash can next to the coffee bar area. "And I didn't go in."

"Why on earth not?"

"'Cause she was crying. I don't do well with crying women. Just ask my wife." Jason shrugged. "I asked Janie, and she confirmed that Amy was doing okay."

Keith dropped the diaper bag and shoved Carter into Jason's arms. "Here. Practice." Then he rushed to Amy's room.

He pushed the door open. "Ams?"

Sniffing met his ears.

"Ams, you okay?" His heart shattered to pieces at the pitiful sound. He moved into the room and got his first full look at her.

"I—I'm fine." She wiped hopelessly at the tears spilling down her cheeks.

Keith lowered himself onto the edge of her bed. "Honey, you're not fine. Talk to me. Please."

She dipped her head, refusing to meet his gaze. She picked at a thread on the hem of the bedsheet.

He placed a finger under her chin and lifted. "Are you in pain?"

"Yes. But that's not it." More tears welled in her sapphire eyes.

He grabbed a handful of tissues and mopped her face. "Then what is it?"

"You left me." She hiccupped a sob.

"Oh, honey. I'm so sorry. I had only planned to be gone a few minutes, but it took longer than I thought it would."

"It doesn't matter." Her defeated tone tugged at his heart.

"It matters to me." He gathered her hands in his. "Honey, talk to me."

"You disappeared a year ago, then you left me again." Tears continued to streak down her face.

Keith pulled more tissues from the boxes and placed them in her hand. "I'm sorry I went missing from your life after my poor judgment with Stacey, but I was ashamed. I knew you'd see through me, and you'd be able to tell what had happened." He shook his head. How could he have thought hiding would solve his problem? He should have manned up from the beginning. He scooped up her hand and held it between his. "If only I could go back and put aside my selfish behavior. I can't change that. But I promise I'm here to stay."

She tilted her head as if considering his words. "Then why did you leave me? You promised to stay."

"I went to get Carter. I thought he might cheer you up."

Her sad smile tore at his heart. "Where is he?"

"In the waiting area with Jason." He brushed the hair from her forehead and inhaled. No better time to start groveling than now. "Ams, please forgive my behavior with your sister. The last thing I ever wanted was to hurt you."

"You made your choice. I have to accept that," Amy mumbled and looked everywhere but at him.

"What do you mean?" Confusion rattled around in his brain. What choice had he made, other than a bad one?

"Nothing."

"Not nothing." The light bulb clicked. Her comments since this whole insane thing with Sheila had begun slapped him across the face. "Oh, Ams. You think I wanted Stacey over you?" He closed his eyes. So many things became clear. "Honey." He dipped his head to meet her eye to eye. "I've only ever wanted you."

"What?" The line between her brows deepened.

"I've loved you since forever. You have always been the twin that I wanted." He cupped her face.

"Me? But Stacey… Carter."

"Sweetheart, that night with Stace was a huge mistake. You're the one I want. Have always wanted. I love you, Ams. Only you."

"You love me?"

"Yes, honey. You." Keith leaned in, careful with her injuries, and touched his lips to hers.

She lifted her arms and pulled him closer, deepening the kiss.

He pulled back, breathless. The underlying passion behind their embrace soothed his brittle self-respect. "Does this mean you forgive me?"

Amy's hoarse laugh filled him with hope. She grabbed her side and turned serious. "I'll admit, you hurt me when I found out about you and Stace. But it wasn't about you. It was about me and my self-esteem. I'm working on that." Her fingers laced the hair at the back of his neck. "And I'm going to have to find a way to put it in the past, because I love you, too."

His heart soared as his mind registered her words. She loved him.

A knock had him twisting to see who had interrupted their moment.

"Hey, I have a little guy who wants in on part of the action." His partner placed Carter in Keith's arms. The lopsided smile on Jason's lips said that he'd witnessed the heated kiss.

"Don't say it." Keith gave Jason a playful glare.

His partner held his palms up with a look that said, *Who me?*

"Knock, knock." Melanie stepped into the room along with Sheriff Monroe. "We wanted to see how you're doing." When Mel's gaze landed on their laced hands, her face lit with excitement.

Dennis plopped down in the chair next to the

bed. Fatigue lined his features. The man hadn't stopped since Sheila's arrest. "Happy to see you awake and talking."

"I'm alive, thanks to all of you," Amy whispered.

"Let's try not to focus on what happened for a bit. My heart is still recovering from seeing the gun to your head." Keith lifted her hand and kissed her knuckles.

"Deal."

A *tap tap* sounded on the hospital room door.

Mayor Taylor peeked in. "Thought we heard voices. Mind if we come in?" Nolan and his son stepped into the room. "I want to apologize for my wife's actions. Please, believe me when I say I had no idea what she had done."

Keith glanced at Amy, and she nodded. "We believe you. Sheila surprised all of us."

"Thank you. She will pay for her actions. I will not stand in the way of that." The mayor rubbed the back of his neck. "I still can't believe this all started because she hated my daughter."

"So it's true, Debbie was your daughter?" Dennis leaned forward, elbows on his knees.

"Yes. I didn't know about her for years. When I discovered the truth, Debbie and I chose to keep it quiet. Neither of us wanted the publicity. I figured the least I could do was give her a job." He smiled. "One that she was pretty good at. I decided not to tell Sheila. My mistake. If I had, maybe all this wouldn't have happened."

Trevor put an arm around his father. "You can't know that." The young man turned his attention to Keith and Amy. "After Sheriff Monroe told us about the leak at Eagle Bay PD, Dad asked me to do some digging. Come to find out, my mom…" He cleared the emotion from his throat. "My mom's cousin Devin works as a 9-1-1 operator there. They discovered he was in on the whole thing. He falsified the records. She was blackmailing him into helping her. Guess she's done it more than once on other things, too."

Jason pursed his lips. "That explains how your call got erased, Amy."

"EBPD is doing a full investigation into Devin, but they told me they found proof that he sent the fake email to Detective Jefferies and was the one who ransacked Amy's house, as well." Trevor shifted his attention to Sheriff Monroe. "The chief of police said he'd keep you in the loop."

"I appreciate that. And thanks for looking into it for us. It answers several questions."

Mayor Taylor patted his son's arm. "Let's let Ms. Baker get some rest." The two exited the room.

After a round of goodbyes, the rest of the crew left as well, leaving Keith alone with Amy and Carter.

His son held out his arms to Amy. The gesture made Keith's insides warm. "Feel like holding him?"

"Sure." Amy gingerly shifted on the bed to make room.

He propped his son next to her.

Time to get back to their conversation. He had to know for sure that Amy wanted the same dream of a future together that he did.

"Before we were so rudely interrupted…" He smirked.

Amy held her finger to his lips. "I meant everything I said." She could read him better than he thought.

"That's what I wanted to hear." He ran a knuckle down his son's chubby cheek. "What do you think, Carter? Should your momma give me a chance?"

The baby babbled as if answering Keith's question.

Amy chuckled and flashed him a grin. "I can't say no to my two guys."

Keith leaned over his happy son and kissed Amy on the top of her head. "I love you, Ams. I always have."

EPILOGUE

Orange and red hues filled the evening sky. Amy stood on Keith's back porch, contemplating the events of the past month.

Her injuries had healed enough that they were down to a dull ache. Mayor Taylor had kept his promise and hadn't put up bail for Sheila. She currently sat in jail, awaiting her trial. Ian had bought a two-bedroom house a few blocks away and insisted Amy live there until her life settled down. She knew, of course, the offer had something to do with wanting his grandson close by. She smiled. Grandpa Ian loved spoiling Carter, and Amy let him.

She and Keith had dated, if one could call it that, for the past four weeks. He'd insisted she stay at his place so his father and he could take care of her. She'd moved into the little home ten days ago. But she and Carter spent every waking moment with Keith when he wasn't on duty.

A couple of weeks ago, Amy bought a new camera and ventured out several times to take pictures for the Eagle Bay Gallery. Once word had gotten out about her ordeal, people had flocked to the shop, buying her landscape photos at a shocking rate. At her last visit, the owner had shooed her out the door with orders to supply him with twenty new masterpieces within the next few weeks.

Her career back on track, her future with Carter and Keith on solid ground, life was good.

Arms wrapped around her from behind. She rested her head on Keith's chest. "Hi."

"Hi back." Keith leaned around and captured her lips.

"Hmm. That's nice."

He chuckled. "I'm glad you think so."

She sobered, thinking about how close they came to messing up and losing the chance to be together. Her lack of self-confidence and his shame had almost derailed their chance at love. But not anymore. They'd promised to be honest with each other and not hide behind insecurities.

"I miss Stace." Amy had no idea why the grief hit her while she stood in his arms. But it had.

"Me, too." Keith's mouth came down on hers, wiping away her sorrow. He pulled back and gazed into her eyes. "But I've only ever wanted you. Never question that."

"Okay." What else could she say since her world spun on its axis in the most wonderful way?

"I love you, Ams."

"Ditto, superhero."

"Ooh, superhero, I kinda like that."

She pivoted and smacked him in the chest. "You're hopeless."

His smile vanished, and his shoulders rose and fell.

Something was wrong.

"Keith? What is it? You're scaring me."

Heart racing, he turned Amy to face him. They'd only dated four weeks, but a lifetime of friendship should count for something. Right?

He sucked in a lungful of air. "Amy."

Her eyes widened.

He'd scared her. Had given her reason to doubt.

"I'm doing this all wrong." He swallowed. "We've known each other going on forever. I know I've messed up. The tiny guy inside with his grandpa is proof of that. I'm so sorry that I hurt you. Although, I'm not sorry Stace and my actions gave us Carter. I love that little dude."

Amy cupped Keith's cheek. "I admit, it was awful, but I agree. Carter was worth the pain."

He nodded, giving himself a moment to control his emotions. He reached into his pocket, pulled out his mother's diamond ring and dropped to one knee.

Amy gasped. Her hand flew to her chest.

"If this is a bad idea, tell me now."

She shook her head. "Go ahead."

"I have loved you since we were twelve. Yes, I made a mistake, but you're the one I want to spend the rest of my life with. The only one I've ever wanted." He took her hands in his. "Ams, will you marry me and be my wife and Carter's mother forever?"

Tears spilled over her lashes. "Yes," she whispered.

"Honey, can you say that again? I don't think I heard you." He'd thought she'd said yes, but the blood whooshing in his ears made it impossible to know for sure.

"Yes."

He breathed a sigh of relief. With a shaky hand, he slid the ring onto her finger. "I love you, Ams. Forever."

He rose, wrapped his arms around his fiancée and sealed his commitment with a kiss. A kiss filled with forgiveness and love.

* * * * *

*If you enjoyed this story,
be sure to pick up
the first book in Sami A. Abrams's
Deputies of Anderson County miniseries,
Buried Cold Case Secrets.
Available now from Love Inspired Suspense!*

Dear Reader,

Thank you so much. Words cannot express how much I appreciate you reading Keith and Amy's story.

When Keith came to life in *Buried Cold Case Secrets*, I knew he had to have his own story. He's such a great guy and needed his happily-ever-after. I loved seeing Keith and Amy move past their poor choices and hurt to find acceptance and love. And isn't Carter the cutest thing ever?

I'd like to send a special shout-out to the Suspense Squad, my peeps, my sisters in crime. They are the best. Knowing there's a group of writers who I can call at any time for writing help or just to laugh is amazing. Thank you, ladies. You're awesome!

I hope you enjoyed reading Keith and Amy's story as much as I did writing it. I'd love to hear from you. You can contact me through my website at samiaabrams.com, where you can sign up for my newsletter to receive exclusive subscriber giveaways.

Hugs,
Sami A. Abrams

COUNTRY LEGACY COLLECTION

EMMETT
Diana Palmer

COURTED BY THE COWBOY

THE RANCHER AND THE BABY

Cowboys, adventure and romance await you in this new collection! Enjoy superb reading all year long with books by bestselling authors like Diana Palmer, Sasha Summers and Marie Ferrarella!

YES! Please send me the **Country Legacy Collection**! This collection begins with 3 FREE books and 2 FREE gifts in the first shipment. Along with my 3 free books, I'll also get 3 more books from the **Country Legacy Collection**, which I may either return and owe nothing or keep for the low price of $24.60 U.S./$28.12 CDN each plus $2.99 U.S./$7.49 CDN for shipping and handling per shipment*. If I decide to continue, about once a month for 8 months, I will get 6 or 7 more books but will only pay for 4. That means 2 or 3 books in every shipment will be FREE! If I decide to keep the entire collection, I'll have paid for only 32 books because 19 are FREE! I understand that accepting the 3 free books and gifts places me under no obligation to buy anything. I can always return a shipment and cancel at any time. My free books and gifts are mine to keep no matter what I decide.

☐ 275 HCK 1939   ☐ 475 HCK 1939

Name (please print)

Address   Apt. #

City   State/Province   Zip/Postal Code

Mail to the **Harlequin Reader Service:**
IN U.S.A.: P.O. Box 1341, Buffalo, NY 14240-8571
IN CANADA: P.O. Box 603, Fort Erie, Ontario L2A 5X3